The Trouble with Happiness

ALSO BY TOVE DITLEVSEN

The Trouble with Happiness

AND OTHER STORIES

TOVE DITLEVSEN

Translated from the Danish by MICHAEL FAVALA GOLDMAN

FARRAR, STRAUS AND GIROUX | NEW YORK

Farrar, Straus and Giroux
120 Broadway, New York 10271

Printed in the United States of America
Originally published in Danish in 1952 and 1963 by Hasselbalch,
    Denmark, as *Paraplyen* and *Den onde lykke*
English translation first published in 2022 by Penguin
    Random House, Great Britain
English translation published in the United States by Farrar,
    Straus and Giroux
First American edition, 2022

Several of these stories previously appeared, in slightly different form, in the
following publications: *Apple Valley Review* ("The Knife"), *The Bangalore Review*
("The Trouble with Happiness"), *Hunger Mountain Review* ("Evening"),
Meat for Tea: The Valley Review ("The Cat" and "The Little Shoes"),
The New Yorker ("The Umbrella")

Library of Congress Cataloging-in-Publication Data
Names: Ditlevsen, Tove Irma Margit, 1917–1976, author. | Goldman, Michael
    (Michael Favala), translator.
Title: The trouble with happiness: and other stories / Tove Ditlevsen ; translated
    from the Danish by Michael Favala Goldman.
Description: First American edition. | New York : Farrar, Straus and Giroux, 2022. |
    "Originally published in Danish in 1952 and 1963 by Hasselbalch, Denmark, as
    'Paraplyen' and 'Den onde lykke'"
Identifiers: LCCN 2021059687 | ISBN 9780374605605 (hardcover)
Subjects: LCSH: Ditlevsen, Tove Irma Margit, 1917–1976—Translations into
    English. | LCGFT: Short stories.
Classification: LCC PT8175.D5 T76 2022 | DDC 839.813/72—dc23/eng/20211217
LC record available at https://lccn.loc.gov/2021059687

Our books may be purchased in bulk for promotional, educational,
or business use. Please contact your local bookseller or the Macmillan
Corporate and Premium Sales Department at 1-800-221-7945, extension 5442,
or by email at MacmillanSpecialMarkets@macmillan.com.

www.fsgbooks.com
www.twitter.com/fsgbooks • www.facebook.com/fsgbooks

10   9   8   7   6   5   4   3   2   1

Contents

BOOK ONE

The Umbrella

The Umbrella

Helga had always – unreasonably – expected more from life than it could deliver. People like her live among us, not differing conspicuously from those who instinctively settle their affairs and figure out precisely how, given their looks, their abilities and their environment, they can do what they need to do in the world. With respect to these three factors, Helga was only averagely equipped. When she was entered in the marriage market, she was a slightly too small and slightly too drab young woman, with narrow lips, a turned-up nose, and – her only promising feature – a pair of large, questioning eyes, which an attentive observer might have called 'dreamy'. But Helga would have been embarrassed if anyone had asked her what she was dreaming about.

She had never demonstrated a special talent of any kind. She had done adequately in public school and had shown good longevity at her domestic jobs. She didn't mind working hard; in her family, that was as natural as breathing. For the most part she was accommodating and quiet, without being withdrawn. In the evenings she went out to dance halls with a couple of girlfriends. They each had a soda and looked for partners. If they sat for a long time without being asked, her girlfriends grew eager to dance with anyone at all, even a man with a hunchback. But Helga just stared absent-mindedly around the venue, and if she saw a man who appealed to her – those who did always had dark hair and brown eyes – she gazed at him so steadily, unguarded and serious, that he could not help but notice her. If someone other than her chosen one approached her (this didn't actually happen very often), she looked down at her lap, blushed slightly and awkwardly excused herself: 'I don't dance.' A few tables away, a pair of brown eyes observed this unusual sight. Here was a girl who wasn't going to fall for the first man who came along.

Over time, many small infatuations rippled the surface of her mind, like the spring breeze that made new leaves tremble without changing their life's course. The man would follow her home and kiss a pair of cold, closed lips, which refused to be opened in any kind of submission. Helga was very conventional. It wasn't that she wouldn't surrender before marriage, but she had it in her head that she would have a ring on and present the chosen man to her parents before it came to that. The ones who were too impatient, or not interested enough to wait for this ceremony, went away more or less disappointed. Sometimes she felt a little pang at those moments, but she soon forgot about it in her life's rhythm of work, sleep, and new evenings with new possibilities.

That was until, at the age of twenty-three, she met Egon. He fell in love with her singularity – that indefinable quality which only a few noticed and even fewer judged an asset.

Egon was a mechanic who was interested in soccer, playing the numbers, pool, and girls. But since every love-struck individual is brushed by wingbeats from a higher level of the atmosphere, it so happened that this commonplace person started reading poetry and expressing himself in ways that would have made his buddies at the shop gape in wonder if they had heard him. Later he looked back on this time as if he had caught a severe illness which left its mark on him for the rest of his life. But as long as it lasted, he was proud and delighted by Helga's carefully preserved chastity, and when they had put on rings and the presentation to her family was over, he took ownership of his property on the prepared divan in his rented room. Everything was how it was supposed to be. She hadn't tricked him. Satisfied, he fell asleep, leaving Helga in a rather confused state. She cried a bit, because here, in particular, she had been expecting something extraordinary. Her tears were pointless, since her path had now been determined. The wedding date was set, supplies were gathered, and she had given notice at her job, because Egon wouldn't have her 'scrubbing other people's floors' after they were married. Her friends were appropriately jealous, and her parents were content. Egon was a skilled laborer, and therefore slightly higher up in the world than her father, who had taught her never to lower herself in this world, but not to 'cook up fantasies', either.

That evening, Helga had no clear premonition that something fateful was happening to her. Even so, she lay awake for a long time, without thinking of anything in particular. When she was half-asleep, a strange desire came drifting into her consciousness: If only I had an umbrella, she thought. It occurred to her suddenly that this item, which for certain people was just a natural necessity, was something she had dreamed of her whole life. As a child she had filled her Christmas wish-lists with sensible, affordable things: a doll, a pair of red mittens, roller skates. And then, when the gifts were lying under the tree on Christmas Eve, she'd been gripped by an ecstasy of expectation. She'd looked at her boxes as if they held the meaning of life itself, and her hands shook as she opened them. Afterward, she'd sat crying over the doll, the mittens, and the roller skates she had asked for. 'You ungrateful child,' hissed her mother. 'You always ruin it for us.' Which was true, because the next Christmas the scene would repeat itself. Helga never knew what she was expecting to find inside those festive-looking packages. Maybe she had once written 'umbrella' on her wish-list and not received one. It would have been ridiculous to give her such a trivial and superfluous thing. Her mother had never owned an umbrella. You took the wind and the weather as it came, without imagining that you could indulgently protect your precious hair and skin from the rain, which spared nothing else.

Helga eventually turned her attention to her role as a fiancée, and, together with her mother, carried out the customary obligations. Yet sometimes she would lie awake next to Egon, or in her bed in the maid's room in the house where she worked, nursing her peculiar dream of owning an umbrella.

A certain image started to form in her mind, which gave her secret desire a forbidden and irresponsible tinge, and cast a delicate, impalpable veil over her expression throughout the day, causing her fiancé to exclaim, with jealousy and irritation, as if he suspected her of some kind of infidelity, 'What are you thinking about?' Once, she answered, 'I'm thinking about an umbrella.' And, with convincing seriousness, he said, 'You're crazy!' By then he had already stopped reading poetry, and he never mentioned her 'dreamy eyes' anymore, which didn't mean that he was disappointed in any way. It was just that now she was a permanent part of his life and routine. She sat through countless soccer matches with him, without ever grasping what it was about this particular form of entertainment that made people shout hurray or fall silent as if possessed.

The image that arose from her memory was this: she was about ten, sitting in the window of the family bedroom, looking down into the courtyard, which was illuminated with a weak glow by the light over the back stairs. She was in her nightgown, and should have been in bed, but she had developed the habit, before going to sleep, of sitting there for a few minutes and staring out into the night without thinking about anything, while a gentle peace erased the events of the day from her mind. Suddenly, she saw the gate open, and across the wet cobblestones of the courtyard, onto which raindrops splashed in an excited rhythm, strolled a pretty, dreamlike creature. Her long yellow dress nearly touched the ground, and high above a profusion of silky blond curls floated an umbrella. It was not like the one Helga's grandmother used – round, black and dome-shaped, with a solid handle – but a flat, bright, translucent thing, which seemed to complement the person who carried it, like a butterfly's radiant wings. It was just a brief glimpse, then the courtyard was deserted as before, but Helga's heart was pounding with strange excitement. She ran into the living room where her mother and father were sitting. 'A lady was walking across the courtyard,' she said softly. Then she added, with awe and admiration, 'She had such a nice umbrella!'

She stood there barefoot, blinking into the light. The familiar room, which lacked anything with a comparable essence, now seemed to her cramped and poor. Her mother looked surprised. 'A lady?' she asked. Then the corners of her mouth turned downward, as they often did when something displeased or bothered her. 'It's that girl next door,' she said sharply. 'It's scandalous.' Then Helga's father turned to her with a flash of anger. 'Why the devil are you sitting staring out the window when you should be in bed?' he yelled. 'Get in there and go to sleep.'

She had seen something that she wasn't allowed to see. Something had been let into her world that wasn't there before. After that, every evening – even though she was an obedient child – she crept over to the window to watch the yellow dress drift across the cobblestones, in all kinds of weather, but always with an inexpressibly sweet and secretive air, and always accompanied by that mysterious umbrella, visible or invisible, depending on if it was raining or not. This vision had nothing to do with the sleepy face that appeared in the neighbor's door frame when Helga knocked to borrow a bit of margarine or flour for her mother, who was always short on the most important ingredients when she was making gravy. And it made no noticeable difference when, one day, this neighbor moved away. For a long time, the child still waited at the window for that long, yellow dress and the buoyant, translucent umbrella. When the nightly passage through the darkening courtyard stopped, she just shut her eyes and listened to the rain splashing against something taut and silky and more distant than all her childhood sounds and smells.

Helga and Egon moved into a two-room apartment that was similar to her parents', and it wasn't far away, either. But it was at street level, and an old wish of Helga's was fulfilled, now that she could sit in her own house and look out at the traffic. She had what she'd never had before – time – and, since idleness is the root of all evil (she was easy prey for sayings like that), this gave her a slightly guilty conscience. Not toward the husband who provided for her but just in general. She allowed herself to become a gentle, self-effacing individual;

she exaggerated the few responsibilities she had, and empha-
sized her frequent visits to her parents and their visits to her.
Her in-laws lived in the country, and she wrote to them often,
though she only had met them at her wedding. Her letters –
which contained detailed accounts of how she spent her day
doing domestic duties and got the most out of Egon's salary
for everyone's benefit – always ended monotonously with
these lines: We are both well and hope the same for you. Your
devoted daughter-in-law, Helga.

Every morning she and her mother went shopping, each
with a headscarf and a sturdy shopping bag. Her mother
shopped for the best cuts of meat at the butcher: men who
work hard need a solid meal, she explained. Helga served
'a solid meal' for her husband at precisely six o'clock every
evening. But from the moment he left in the morning until
that hour, she rarely thought of him. When the shopping and
cleaning were done, she sat at the window with some darning that was meant to distract her from the fact that she was
sitting there idly, while the people in the street all seemed to
have so much to do. From her protected, hidden spot behind
the curtain, she observed them with interest and seriousness,
the way she had, before Egon, observed all men with brown
eyes. She was filled with vague curiosity: Where were they
going? Why were they so busy? Although she didn't realize it,
she was lonely. She often thought about her mother, because,
in Helga's eyes, she was a person, unlike everyone else, who
never changed. It was a kind of respite for Helga to be with
her mother. Mother and child. Comfort. She loved recalling
her childhood. She liked hearing her mother talk about things
that had happened. Her mother talked a lot. The sentences
streamed from her, forming sturdy frames around distant,
blurry landscapes. Often she said, 'You are doing so well. You

9

should appreciate it more, but you always have been ungrateful.' 'Ungrateful how?' Helga asked. Then she always got the story about all the tears she had shed when she received gifts. 'In the end, we were simply afraid to buy you anything,' her mother said. And there in the twilight they sat, shaking their heads at the thought of this unappreciative child who had cried over gifts that would have delighted other children. They talked about this mystery in the same tone one might use to talk about getting over scarlet fever: Good heavens, you were so sick, we thought you might never get over it!

Most of all, Helga loved hearing about everything that was outside the parameters of her own memory: about the first words she'd spoken, when she'd been toilet-trained, and so on – things that did not differentiate her at all from any other child a mother might talk about. Her mother liked to end these stories by getting up and gathering her belongings as she remarked: Well, we won't be seeing those times again, or some similar generalization spoken in a tone devoid of complaint, but that left a small rip in the veil that lay over Helga's innermost being, like the membrane around an unborn child.

When her mother left (always just before Egon was expected home) and Helga waved to her familiar substantial figure for as long as she could see it, then she sat back down at the window without turning on the light. A sadness grew within her and around her. She thought: If only Egon would come home. But when he did come, and filled the small rooms with his noisy company, every enchantment was shattered. Could it be that it wasn't him she was longing for? She walked around quietly, carrying out her housewifely duties, picked at her food like a bird, and said 'yes' and 'no', when her husband's remarks required an answer. Once, he regarded her closely. 'You should have a kid,' he said. 'I damn well don't understand why it's not happening.' Then she blushed, partly at her deficiency in that department, but more because she didn't actually mind not having a child. Her togetherness with her mother allowed the child Helga to live on within her, so it was as if there wasn't room for another one. Sometimes she lied to Egon when he asked if her mother had been over, because for some reason he didn't like her mother to visit so often when he wasn't home.

The days passed without much to distinguish one from the next.

One evening Helga had the food waiting for an hour before Egon came home, and when he did arrive, he was drunk. He threw himself down on the divan, from which he followed her movements through the living room with a watchful, sinister glare. 'What's wrong with you?' he asked suddenly. 'Your face looks all pasty.' She was shocked and quickly put some rouge on her cheeks, but later she got used to his tone. She also got used to making food that was easily reheated, because it became impossible to predict when he would come home. She told her mother about it. 'Egon started drinking.' Her mother seemed to be more uneasy about it than Helga was. 'When a man drinks, it's because he's dissatisfied with his wife,' she declared. And, since she was of the opinion that you could always do something about a problem, she advised her daughter to 'talk it out' with Egon and figure out what was the matter. But Helga had never tried to put herself in another person's shoes; it had never been necessary. Her entire character consisted of a pile of memories without a pattern or a plan. There were a number of pairs of brown eyes, a twilight mood, an immense, undefined expectation, a yellow dress, and an umbrella. There were tears and disappointments, and so many other things, and small joys in between. And there was a man who had opened her pale, narrow lips, and for a few moments made her feel the tug of something unknown and wonderful. There was a voice that had said strange and sweet words to her, and over it all stretched the fine silk umbrella canopy of her childhood and her dreams. This had nothing to do with the man who had started drinking. She thought she had given him as much of herself as he could reasonably expect, and her vague feeling of inadequacy with him was only because she wasn't pregnant, as a newly married wife ought to be. But it seemed to her that, as usual, she expected something more for herself, a kind of surfeit that went only to other, unknown individuals. Not that she blamed anyone for anything – she had never done that, because she knew how unreasonable she was. She had written things on her life's wish-list which were achievable: time to dream, a husband with brown eyes, and a child – the last one for conventional reasons. Her outward behavior had always been dictated by tangible things, so she assumed that it was something concrete that had made Egon start drinking and speaking harshly to her. She nodded thoughtfully to her mother over her tea and promised to 'talk it out' with her husband. But she had already decided it was the lack of a child that was bothering him, and matters no one could do anything about were not proper topics of conversation. Not even with her mother.

That evening Egon came home at midnight. He threw his dirty overalls in the middle of the living room and called for Helga, who was warming up the food.

'I'm fed up to here with it,' he said slowly, swaying on his legs like a sailor. She appeared in the kitchen door, staring at him with her sorrowful, wondering eyes.

'What are you fed up with?' she asked anxiously.

'Everything,' he said, his alcohol breath reeking in her face. 'What do you think I am, an idiot?'

She didn't answer, but pulled back from him a step. Her mind was slow, never fully able to follow a situation, especially a surprising one. Her mind quickened only with memories.

'The food is burning,' she said hesitantly.

He laughed callously.

'I don't want any food,' he drawled. 'I ate already.'

'Where did you eat?' she asked quietly, starting to untie her apron. Her hands trembled slightly. He could see that she was hurt or afraid, and he laughed loudly again.

'With a good-looking girl, if you absolutely must know,' he shouted triumphantly. Then he belched in her face, walked into the bedroom and lay down on the bed, fully dressed.

Helga followed him. She looked at him, confused, numb to any clear thought or feeling, as she fumbled for a safe, child-like footing. She whispered, 'I'm going to tell my mother.' But he was already asleep.

Actually, she didn't feel any more hurt by the thought that he had very likely cheated on her than she knew a person *ought* to feel. A husband shouldn't drink, but, if he cheats, that is much worse. Instead of having her usual fantasies, she imagined him with another woman, but it really didn't make much difference. It was only her outer life that he was threatening. It didn't change who she was; her body was the same as before, only with the small difference that it had lessened in value to other men. The words 'other men' hadn't occurred to her since she'd got married. Now, as she slowly undressed, she thought only about that, because she knew that her mother would. Her mother would rationalize that if this husband neglected his obligations to her daughter, then she would have to turn to other men with brown eyes for

the pursuit of her daily bread – this idea, that the men absolutely had to have brown eyes, in fact came from her mother.
A remark that had stuck: Dark men are goodness itself.

Egon slept heavily beside her, and Helga lay observing him.
Despite the late hour, she wasn't sleepy. His chin was relaxed,
he had a beard, and he was snoring. This was how one might
think about a stranger, not one's husband. Maybe he had been
a stranger to her for quite some time – ever since the day she
had gone to him with such high expectations, and departed
with such deep disappointment, in her own quiet way, without acknowledging it as any great calamity. What does one
person mean to another anyway, except when one forces the
other to act?

Helga's reaction was strange. The times when she'd stolen
a small amount of the household money and concealed it
in a little box, originally a jewelry box that she had been given
for her confirmation, she hadn't had any particular purpose in
mind. Perhaps she had tried to convince herself that it was for
Christmas gifts or other things they would struggle to afford.
But now she realized why she had saved this money. She smiled
suddenly in the dark, and very quietly slipped out of bed and
walked to the drawer where she had hidden the box. The
moon lit the little room like a false dawn. With the deftness
of a thief, she counted the money. There were almost forty
kroner. She held them in her hands, smiling gently, redeemed
and alone, like a child smiling in her sleep. All she could think
of was an open, translucent umbrella with a certain shape and
color. She longed for the morning, and her heart pounded
fast, the way a woman's heart pounds when she is going to
meet her lover. She imagined the street in the rain, and herself
wandering beneath this silken canopy. Vague, bright images
spread like dandelion tufts across her mind: a house where

she had worked, the wife in a dinner dress: Oh, Helga, bring me my umbrella. She had held many umbrellas in her hand without thinking about them. Things outside her world didn't really mean anything to her. Until now. Until she acted.

She slipped back into bed, and her husband reached for her body in his sleep, mumbling something she couldn't make out. Carefully she laid his limp hand back under the comforter, as a hint of a distant tenderness flowed through her. For a second, she felt as much searing emotion as she could ever feel for another person, not including her mother. Recently, Egon had often yelled about getting a divorce, said that he wasn't going to stay married to a broom handle, but words slung at her that way passed right through her as through a sieve. Her parents had always yelled like that when they fought. It didn't mean anything, and she was used to it. All that mattered to her was that the neighbors didn't hear. She was never much for arguing; she just figured that other people were so inclined, and she wasn't. She defended herself in another fashion. There was no way of knowing when it would surface. Maybe Egon had never cheated on her at all, but that didn't matter anymore.

The next morning they both acted as if nothing had happened. That was how their lives were. Helga made her husband's lunch, made him coffee, and kissed him on the cheek as he left. Exactly as usual. Then she went shopping, filled with light, expectant thoughts. And there was no one to tell her that she looked beautiful that morning, in the way that perfectly regular people can, once in a while, when they are feeling happy. She brightened the November day like a pale, delicate morning star, trembling gently and devotedly before it is extinguished. She wasn't the same person that she had been the day before. She was a woman walking into shops looking at umbrellas. It took a long time to find the right one. And she carried it awkwardly on the way home, like a man who isn't used to carrying a bouquet of flowers.

Once she was inside, she opened the umbrella and skipped around the apartment with it. Her joy was pristine. She walked just like the woman in the yellow dress from her childhood. She walked past piles of dirty dishes, through large, bright rooms with palm trees in the corners and paintings on the walls. She entered an illuminated ballroom and remembered her first dance. She lifted the hem of her invisible dress and danced a few steps. The shaft of the umbrella was cool, thin, and strong, something to hold tightly, something to admire, to believe in, to acknowledge. Now she could say to her girlfriends: I bought an umbrella. And it would still be all hers. She shut it, studying the way it functioned: the shiny ribs, the tiny, adorable silk buttons, and the durable yet translucent cloth, against which the rain would someday thrum its melody of forgotten and lost times.

Her ecstasy lasted most of the day. She didn't think about her mother, she didn't clean, she didn't even dust the furniture. She didn't think about Egon either.

When he returned, unexpectedly, straight from work, she was sitting in the window at her usual spot, with the darning basket, which was empty, in front of her. She smiled at him and stood up.

'I haven't made any dinner,' she said offhandedly, adding as a provocation, which was unlike her, 'I thought maybe you would be eating out.'

He didn't answer, and she ascertained that he was sober, and that he was trying to avoid her eyes. Why? She wanted to tell him about the umbrella and her little swindle. She needed to share her joy with someone. But he looked so terribly ceremonious as he sat himself at the table and cleared his throat. 'I'm sorry about yesterday,' he said awkwardly. 'It wasn't true. I was just drunk.'

'I see,' she said flatly. All day she hadn't given one thought to what had happened the day before. Even now it was strangely difficult for her to think about anything other than the umbrella, but the situation demanded that she say something. She felt embarrassed, as he did, and she stared down at her hands.

'That's all right,' she said truthfully. 'I've forgotten all about it.'

She didn't notice the shadow darkening his face, and she didn't register how despairingly he tensed his whole body toward her. She was a person who didn't come when she was called. She was the one who called when she needed something, in a thin voice, which was easily drowned out by the storm. Besides, it is very rare that two people call at the same time and both get responses. She was content in herself – she even had a bit extra to share – but her husband had pursued her for a long time like a big clumsy animal, while she, agile and light as a scared gazelle, had run from him into a bright, hidden clearing in the woods.

She sat down across from him, small and erect, and again seemed to him both secretive and alluring. As he had a long time ago, he asked jealously and fearfully: 'What are you thinking about?' And, just like back then, her clear, dreamy eyes glided over him as she responded, 'An umbrella.' And then, with sudden animation, 'I bought it, Egon. Do you want to see it?' She was already skipping to the entryway, breathless with excitement.

But he followed behind her and suddenly, angrily, pulled the fine object from her hands and broke it in half over his strong knee.

'There's your umbrella!' he shouted, and she stood for a second in shock, staring at the pieces, at the cleverly formed ribs, and the torn silk.

Then she walked silently past him into the little living room, back to the manageable, the tolerable, the predetermined. She sat by the window as before, finally realizing that this was her place, and that everything was the way it was supposed to be. The colors in her memory mixed together, forming the beginning of a kind of pattern. She realized that she could never be the owner of an umbrella. It was only natural – it made sense that it was ruined. She had set herself up against the secret law steering her inner world. Few people, even once in their lives, dare to make the inexpressible real.

Helga smiled distantly at her husband. It was as if he had suddenly caused some string inside her to vibrate slightly, maybe because he had shown her the limits of her potential before it flowed out into nothingness. She didn't think about it like that. She just thought: This is exactly as if I had cheated on him, and he's forgiven me. And she nodded, seriously and absently, as if to a child who wants to take a star down from the sky and give it away, when he, intensely occupied with screwing a new bulb into the ceiling fixture, said to her over his shoulder:

'You'll get another umbrella.'

The Cat

They sat across from one another on the train, and there was nothing special about either of them. They weren't the kind of people your eyes would land on if you tired of staring at the usual scenery, which appears to rush toward the train from a distance and then stand still for a second, creating a calm picture of soft green curves and little houses and gardens, whose leaves vibrate and turn grayish in the smoke streaming back from the train like a long billowing pennant. You wouldn't guess if they were married or not, whether they had children, how old they were, their occupations, et cetera, just to pass the time. You could see marriage and office work in their expressionless eyes. The man hid his face behind the newspaper, and the woman appeared to have fallen asleep. They sat there every morning and evening, at the times office and factory workers commute. Usually in the same seats in the last train car. Recently there had been a few days when she wasn't there. Maybe she'd been sick. So he had sat alone, and to an observer it didn't make any difference. He had spread his newspaper wide and read it carefully, folded it together neatly, and left it on the seat when he got off. A completely regular office worker in his thirties. It was the cold time of year, so maybe she had had the flu.

He lightly touched her knee. 'We're here,' he said.

It wasn't necessary, because she wasn't sleeping. She got up and took her bag out of the baggage holder, straightened her hat and walked in front of him off the train. He looked at her from the side as they continued down the road toward home. She appeared tired; she always did. She wasn't sick, and she didn't do any more than other women who worked while simultaneously taking care of their houses – less, in fact, since they had no children. But she had taken on the attitude that she carried the burdens of the world. At least that's how it seemed to him, and it bothered him. Recently he had been easily irritated. He tautened his lips to a narrow line and cleared his throat:

'Is the cat still at our house?' he asked.

'I think so,' she said. 'I wasn't going to chase it out into this freezing cold.'

He wrinkled his brow and grew silent. The animal had slowly sneaked into their lives. They had come home one evening to find it meowing outside their door. So she had given it a bit of milk and sent it off. The next morning it was back, and he threw a rock at it when they left. But in the evening she let it inside, because it was below freezing, and it seemed to have no other place to go. In the morning the entire house smelled of cat urine; the creature wasn't even housebroken. It purred apologetically at their legs, and she ran around cleaning up after it, spraying ammonia to get rid of the smell.

Then disagreements started over the cat. He let it out, and she let it back in. When they lay in bed in the evening, they heard the faint meowing outside their front door, and she got up to give it something to eat, while an incomprehensible resentment arose in her husband. 'Don't let it in,' he yelled to her. But in the morning there it was down in the living room, jumping elegantly up onto her lap. She babied it. 'Little pussycat,' she said, 'if only you were housebroken.' The smell made her face go pale as they sat and drank coffee. While she was in the hospital, he was able to get rid of it. Every time he caught sight of the cat near their house, he threw a rock at it, frustrated that he could never hit it. But when she came home, the first thing she asked about was the cat. She stood outside the house calling, 'Here pussycat, come here, baby. Mommy's home again.' And it actually did come when she called, as if it had been nearby the whole time waiting for her. She scraped the snow away from around the front step and brought the creature into their warm living room. As she put her cheek to its fur she had tears in her eyes. 'You sweet little kitty,' she whispered. He hated sentimentality, and he hated dirt and disorder. She could put her energy and care into other things. Inwardly, he was glad she had had a miscarriage. That child would have turned their lives upside down. Things had progressed so steadily in the six years they had been married. They had a house and nice furniture, fine friends, the boss over for dinner once a month. A child would have meant she would have had to stop working, their standard of living would have gone down, their social standing too. He saw it as something to be avoided, and he tried to get her to see the sense in his reasoning. But she harbored a gentle expectation, living in a dream world where dry numbers and computations did not enter. 'A real live little baby of our own,' she said solemnly. 'The house? It's just a dead thing.'

He had thought she was betraying their mutual efforts; she had withdrawn from him and was alone with this strange, foreign body. It was as if she were getting younger and more beautiful because of it, and he felt a kind of jealousy, because he wasn't part of her happiness. In his childhood home there had been six siblings, and he remembered it as one continuous crying fit and quarrel about money, of which there was never enough. Children make people poor.

When did the cat show up? It must have been right after they realized she was pregnant, but apart from that, the two things had nothing to do with one another. One morning she was sick and was driven to the hospital in great haste; the whole thing only took a few days, and then he felt relieved. It wasn't anyone's fault. If they had had the baby, of course they would have figured it out. But it was better this way. He picked her up from the hospital, with flowers, bought out of a vague sense that she needed consoling. But she didn't really register the flowers, holding them awkwardly and tensely in the car on the way home. She let him pat her hand, but it was like a foreign, dead object in his. 'Did you chase away the cat?' she had asked, and he thought it was a strange question, but women didn't really have a sense of proportion. For a few days he took special care above and beyond the usual. He helped her with the dishes in the evening, and he let the cat come around. Once he even removed its refuse personally. But when she didn't seem to notice his efforts, he stopped and went back to the way he was before. They didn't mention the baby. Just once, while she sat with the cat in her lap, she said, 'So I guess you're happy again?' He defended himself, feeling aggrieved, and over time it seemed to him that in fact he had been the one who wanted to have a baby, and that he was the only one grieving for the loss. Since it didn't work out, he could allow himself to be sad about it. As long as she had her cat, she was happy. But he would put an end to that soon enough. The constant filth.

The smell hit them as soon as they stepped inside. He demonstratively opened all the windows. Now that creature had to go. He kicked it off the chair while she was in the kitchen, and it bolted out to her. He could hear her babbling to it as she poured milk in its saucer. He lay on the divan when she came in with the bucket and ammonia, a scarf around her hair. Cleaning woman, he thought, furious.

But a sudden warmth coursed through him at seeing her bent, flexible back, which surprised him. It had been quite a while. 'Grete?' he said.

'What is it?' She didn't turn around.

'Come over here.'

He got up, standing motionless and abashed before her clear, questioning look. Jesus Christ, he thought, we are married after all. But she walked by him on her sensible flats and suddenly seemed so unreasonably foreign, as if he had never held her in his arms. But it's not my fault, he thought, with a smoldering, helpless anger. Was it my fault it didn't amount to anything?

He stared at the closed door and then noticed the cat under the desk, following him with its predatory stare. It was lying there as if hunting for mice, motionless and in patient suspense. He stood totally still in the middle of the floor, feeling the same preying watchfulness fill his own senses. He took a step toward the creature, which hunched its back and hissed quietly. Then he looked for something to smack it with, but just as he took his eyes off it, the cat raced over and jumped out of one of the open windows. He shut the windows in all three rooms, one after the other, and then walked out to check if the front and kitchen doors were locked. Leaning against the kitchen counter he watched his wife. She was putting meat through the grinder and catching it in her hands, and leading it into a bowl as it came creeping out of the little holes like long, bright worms.

Keeping her eyes on her work, she said, 'Where did the cat go?'

He shrugged: 'How should I know?'

She looked up quickly: 'You let it out,' she said. Her voice trembled slightly with anger.

'Oh, you have cat on the brain,' he said, attempting a laugh.

She washed her hands and dried them carefully, finger by finger, as if she was putting on gloves.

'Go and get it,' she said calmly.

He glanced away. He wanted to say something. There was a lump stuck in his throat, as if he was about to cry. What is the problem? he thought. It's almost like she hates me. With a helpless look he walked past her and out of the kitchen.

'Kitty,' he called. 'Here, kitty.' If the cat comes back, he thought, then everything will be fine. But it didn't come. He searched the yard, and all his anger was chased away by something overwhelming and unknown for which he didn't have the words. He looked between the trees in the snow-covered grass; he was searching for a little cat which brought a load of trouble and no joy; it didn't make any sense. He was a man who always had been led by reason, and who had advanced step by step because of this. He had never had urges to do meaningless things. He had married a pretty girl from a good family; in a few years he would be a manager, and then they might be able to allow themselves to have a child. Grete could stop working – 'Here, Kitty, Kitty' – he pleaded for his life and didn't know why. He was afraid. He was moving in unknown territory; he didn't recognize the woman who was standing in his kitchen anymore, demanding he return with a mangy, untrained cat. He wanted her the way she was before, when he could talk to her about everyday things. He would hold her in his arms and feel the pride of ownership again. Maybe he could buy her with that cat.

It was sitting in a corner of the shed, hissing as he approached. 'Kitty,' he whispered gently. 'Don't be afraid. Come inside to your Mama, come on now.'

It slipped between his legs and jumped in through the open kitchen door all by itself. She had it in her arms when he came in. Tears were falling on its fur. She kissed it on the head, on the paws, and gave it long smacking kisses on its ears. He could see her body trembling. 'Grete,' he said, frightened. Suddenly she let go of the creature, as if she had been awoken from a deep sleep. Then she stared at her hands, which had just been caressing the cat so lovingly. She lifted her head and took a wobbly step toward her husband. Then she stopped and wiped her forehead with the back of her hand.

'Well,' she said, 'I guess I'd better finish making dinner.'

He felt something in his mind soften, and he wanted to go and put his arm around her shoulder, to be close to her in some way. Maybe she expected it; maybe she needed it. But then it occurred to him that the neighbors had probably seen him lying on the ground and crawling around between the bushes, meowing.

He straightened his tie and walked back into the living room. The cat followed, its eyes riveted to him. And though he didn't show it, he was aware of its presence all the time.

My Wife Doesn't Dance

She was on her way toward the door to answer the telephone when she heard her husband's voice – she thought he was napping on the divan, but maybe the telephone had woken him – so she turned around to go back into the kitchen. His words reached her, as if from a distance, through the glass door: *Thank you very much, that's very kind of you, but my wife doesn't dance.*

She stopped and listened, blood rushing to her cheeks, and her heart started hammering as if some danger was approaching. What's wrong? she thought, shaken up. Nothing has happened. Of course he knows I don't dance. Everyone knows I can't. If we're invited out to dance, it's a perfectly natural thing to let them know.

She continued her work in the kitchen, feeling distracted and strangely awkward. She had never tried to hide it from him. It wouldn't have been possible anyway. Ever since he had kissed her for the first time, he must have known, or even before he ever met her. It was something people mentioned whenever her name came up. 'She had childhood paralysis, the poor thing.' But it didn't mean anything to him, apparently – and might that be the real reason she fell in love with him? In his eyes she had never seen any of that horribly considerate sympathy.

She started peeling potatoes with quick, mechanical movements, while at the same time trying to calm herself down: Nothing happened, it was just that I heard it by chance (but would he have said the same thing if I had been in the room?). Who was calling? Maybe an old college buddy who didn't know anything about her. A hollow melancholy enveloped her with an unmerciful darkness she could not escape. Something had changed suddenly, though she couldn't say exactly what it was.

Everyone could see it for themselves, so why should it make any difference that they never talked about it? It followed her everywhere, every day, every minute: on the bus, on the trolley, in the stores, and in the long, long streets, where it was almost impossible to slip unnoticed through an open square or – even worse – past those groups of young people standing on corners after work, whose revealing, watchful eyes tormented her more than anything – but not so much after she had gotten married and therefore was generally recognized as a woman who could be desired and loved, and be someone's partner like anyone else. Did he think about it when they were out together? All the time? Had she lulled herself into a false sense of security here, inside the walls of the home they had created together? Her childhood dream of being like everyone else or just to have any other kind of bodily problem, something that wasn't noticed at first glance – an unhealthy complexion, spindly legs, ugly hands – returned to her. That kind of thing could be hidden for a time, even from the husband she loved. Then one day, perhaps during an argument, she might finally hear that it had been on his mind the whole time. Then she would feel exposed and cry, as if her life and happiness were ruined for all time, even though she could still hide it from those she only came in contact with by chance or infrequently. But a woman who limps doesn't get exposed the same way. She doesn't limp more or less, depending on if anyone mentions it. It is a fact and visible to everyone, like red hair or a harelip. Until now she had never tried to hide it from anyone. And if anyone invited her out to dance, it was only natural that her husband would point out that she didn't do that. Perhaps coolly and without emotion, as if, in response to another question, he were just saying: Our walls are eggshell, the bedroom is blue, and we've been married for about six months. – It doesn't change what is already established. Only children yell 'limpy-gimp' and they only yell it at you when you're a child too.

She had slipped from her childhood torments into the polite and considerate world of adults. She had succeeded in not thinking about what people said about her when she wasn't there. Besides, she had been able to elevate herself in other ways. She could speak on literature, politics, art, and foreign countries as well as any man in their circle. She had lived in France for two years, painting a bit and drawing. She had learned to converse with all kinds of people and to hold her own in any gathering. But did any of this really interest her, apart from as a vehicle to draw people's attention away from other women's well-formed legs and normal gait?

She was done with the potatoes, and as she stood with one hand on the faucet and the other swirling around in the pot, it was as if suddenly she didn't have the strength to rinse the potatoes and put them on the stove. She sat down on a kitchen chair and dried her hands on her apron. There she remained completely still, staring straight ahead, as if she were a machine that could continue working for a minute after the power was shut off, but would then stop with a shudder and go dead, indifferent to the shreds of incomplete work wound between its ingenious gears and cylinders.

Right, everyone knows. With her most intimate girlfriends she could talk about it once in a while – and then at home of course, where it gradually became an inevitability similar to her mother's arthritis and her father's perpetual headaches.

But to *him* she had never mentioned it. Sometimes – especially at the outset of their relationship – she felt that he was just about to mention it, maybe to help her, but then she got up and gave him a kiss or asked about something and turned his thoughts in another direction. Perhaps he had gradually begun to understand that he must never bring it up, because it would ruin her illusion that, at least to one person, she was complete, the most beautiful and most loved woman in the world. In this way she had succeeded in separating this curse from their marriage, from her husband's eyes and consciousness, and thereby from her own thoughts – at least in the time she spent here in the kitchen and in the other rooms – a newly married and happy young couple's first home. She had placed her life's great despair outside the door, and only when she left home did the sorrowful black cape wind back around her. Because out in the world nothing had changed – not the impersonal, telling glances from strangers, nor the brazen staring of children.

But now someone had opened the door, and an invisible and icy cold wind blew around her, around her alone, and only she felt it. She didn't know what she should do, or why she had to do something. But she did. The words still echoed in her ears: *My wife doesn't dance*. She felt a powerless bitterness, as if he had lied on her behalf, as if he had been unfaithful. But that kind of thing would have been easier for her to bear, because it was something that could have happened to anyone, something both she and others could grasp, discuss, and relate to. This she couldn't share with anyone, least of all her husband, who was now sitting in the living room waiting for dinner while reading the daily paper.

A cold hate washed over her. He was sitting there completely unaware, waiting for his evening comfort. Blameless. But if you feel betrayed, you *are* betrayed.

She got up and went back to preparing the meal. She sliced up the meat, made gravy. Hate penetrated her mind like a bright, sharp flame, forcing her thoughts so far from their usual channels that it was as if a completely different woman were standing there from the one who, just half an hour or less before, had gone into the living room to answer the phone. In this cutting, cool light she saw the form of a strange, inconsequential person, who admired her intelligence, enjoyed her food, and venerated her social class, which was above his. How courteously he had approached her parents' large, solid rooms as a working student, striving for entrance into the culture in which she had been born and raised. Had she ever been anything for him other than a means to achieve a lasting separation from the social class to which he belonged? So he accepted the leg in the bargain! Apparently he wasn't able to conquer a girl who was both cultivated *and* graceful.

But hate is just as void of sense as love. Its fire is cold, burning with evil. There was another man, a shadow of him, and she had to try to make him appear in her mind now, the one who had elevated her to the light with his gentle voice and his good, warm hands, protected her, made her forget. He mustn't notice anything. Maybe (with a tiny, futile wisp of hope) in a little while everything could go back to how it was.

She would carry out the food and ask, in a perfectly normal voice, who was on the phone. It would be strange if she didn't ask; it would arouse his suspicions. Suspicions of what? She could say with a little smile: I heard what you said, that I don't dance. But I *can* dance actually, even with the bad leg. Maybe, maybe then everything would be even better than before, when there would no longer be anything between them that they couldn't mention.

And she told herself that he wouldn't love her any more or less than before, since he did marry her, after all – and everyone knows he did it *despite that*. The hate, and its painful and false vision, slowly disappeared. Maybe he had said it that loudly to actually help her? But the thought that he might have known her anxiety about the subject all along filled her with incomprehensible shame, which was more unbearable than everything else.

She drew out her tasks, feeling almost like a dominant enemy was awaiting her, out in the cozy living room. She had to go in and set the table, but how could she look him in the eye and act naturally?

In a panic, she put the meat on the dish, set the plates on the tray, forgot the salt and pepper, and walked down the long hallway, listening for her own footsteps, her limping footsteps, which he now heard approaching, just like every other evening, and yet not like any other.

He put down the newspaper and smiled at her. 'That smells good,' he said. She started setting the table without looking at him. She formed the sentence privately, the difficult, meaningful sentence: I heard the phone; who was it?

She tried to buy herself some time. While we're eating, she thought, while he's occupied with the food – then he won't look at me.

She went out to get the glasses and felt his gaze glide mercilessly over her body, making her movements stiff and awkward, so the shorter, skinny leg hobbled more obviously than usual down the hall. Tears burned her eyes, tears of hate and shame, which could never be alleviated by crying.

When they were sitting across from one another, he cleared his throat as if he were going to say something, and he looked at her, surprised and questioning. Without thinking, in fearful panic, she pushed the water pitcher and it toppled, spilling water all over the tablecloth.

'What are you doing? Wait a second, let me help you.' His voice was friendly, a bit curious, and she let him fetch a rag as she sat motionless, watching him dry the spill carefully, while her heart shrank to a little hard lump. He has no idea, she told herself. He doesn't have any idea what I'm going through. And suddenly she perceived him as a complete stranger, a person she just happened coincidentally to be in the room with, and she was able to feel disconnected from him, from her love for him, her solidarity with him, and she decided again from her profound loneliness to ask who had called – she had already opened her mouth when her eyes met his. His eyes were good-natured, sad, and wise. They were searching penetratingly for something, maybe just a confirmation. Of what? The words stopped at her lips. They would never be spoken.

She smiled sadly and distantly. It's over, she thought. Not yet, not tomorrow. Maybe he'll never know it's over.

'I'm a little tired today,' she said apologetically, and they both started eating, while carefully avoiding looking one another in the eye.

His Mother

The old lady was awaiting a visit. But it's not really accurate to call her a 'lady', although she would certainly find the title appropriate. Because the term 'old lady' automatically brings to mind a lovable, mild-mannered, white-haired woman, or at least a dignified one. But lovable is not the right description; mild-mannered doesn't fit either. And she really is too short, bent, and slovenly to be called dignified. If you happened to see her apart from her dreary, stately furniture in these carpeted rooms with which she has merged, and which soon will be located in her son's bright, new home, looking awkward and being about the only things that miss her, you would simply think: There goes an old woman; or maybe even: There goes a *poor* old woman, because for years she has never spent money on herself, except for that pot of a hat she bought for three kroner last year at a second-hand shop, and the strange dress she got an elderly seamstress to make out of her husband's twenty-year-old overcoat for five kroner (she has a knack for finding cheap labor); and in addition to that, a kind of smock that was made from the lining, with sleeves from an old, moth-eaten curtain. – And she hopes she doesn't have to buy any more clothes in her lifetime; you get nothing for your money these days, and who does she have to dress up for anyway –

It was Sunday, and she was expecting her youngest son, who was a student and actually lived at home, but most nights slept at his friends' houses. He was twenty-seven, and his studies were being drawn out, since his father had died completely unexpectedly and left only the bare minimum to support his widow and nothing at all to his son. So he had to work during the day and study at night. An advance on his inheritance was out of the question. Despite her piousness, his mother hated anything that reminded her that she was going to die one day, and the word 'inheritance' filled her with images of ungrateful children, indecent funeral banquets, powerlessness, and darkness. It was good for him to support himself, she thought. Young people shouldn't have inordinate amounts of free time –

But he still had time for girls, however he managed it.

She carefully whisked a feather duster over her husband's portrait, around which hung a dried wreath of small blue and yellow flowers with shiny beech leaves jutting out. She paused in front of the picture, and for a moment merged so silently and naturally with her surroundings that she seemed closer to death than when she was asleep. Then reality again took hold of her sinewy, though fragile body; she shivered, seeking respite from the relaxed, almost jolly eyes above the pastor's ruff collar. 'Young people don't grasp the seriousness –' she said heavily. 'No humility toward life, no sense of responsibility.'

She was really hoping they could keep their hands off one another until they were married. She would never forget that terrible day when she had found something in the inner reaches of the boy's wallet, something about the use of which there could not be the least doubt, even if one had been married to a pastor and quietly received the children it was God's will they should have. She had waited for him tearfully that evening, with the small, sterile, crinkling package between two fingers. 'Now, Asger, have you sunk so low that you don't trust your mother anymore?'

Her eyes grew dark with anger at the memory, while the porcelain trinket on the desk got a once-over with the duster. Then she lugged a chair beneath the crystal chandelier, and, panting heavily, lifted her dress to reveal a pair of short, thick, bowed legs in black socks. She stepped up onto the chair from which, with the help of a surprising ability to stretch, she sent a rag twisted around the end of a broomstick in the direction of the faintly chiming pendants, allowing her to shake down a bit of dust onto the crocheted table cover that had been placed over the large, round mahogany table for the occasion.

He was supposed to come at three o'clock with his girl-friend. Now it was almost four.

She stepped down gingerly and stood there leaning on the broom handle, looking around the living room to see if there were any more specks of dust visible to her weak eyes. She caught sight of her sister's stern, stiff expression, which from several ages and different photographic projections observed the room from all angles. And she sighed long and deep at the thought of the treatment the poor woman had likely been exposed to at the mental hospital, without anyone ever knowing, because she was no longer able to liberate a single thought from her depression's impenetrable morass. 'Poor little Agnes!' But then her thoughts shifted to this sister's numerous offspring, of which the eldest, whom she hadn't actually seen since he was tiny, was at that moment suffering from a terrible pneumonia; and even though nowadays there were treatments for it, you could never know for sure. God's ways are beyond our comprehension.

The old woman's life was replete with misfortunes, the most recent one always seeming to her the heaviest to bear. She sniffed them out and took them in with real talent. Her family was large, taking into account her siblings' children and the families by marriage. And somewhere along the line there was always a stillborn baby, a grown son who went off the rails, or a daughter who had a child outside of wedlock. And in some magical way she always knew instantly, and every time it pained her deeply and was just as difficult and burdensome. Alas, what we have to go through – it's a good thing Daddy's not alive anymore! It was really remarkable what she could endure. Even the neighbor's sorrows and the other miseries on her periphery, which she uncovered through conversations with salesmen and residents in her building, hit her hard and painfully. But in the end it all merged together, and at heart she didn't feel noticeably worse when her sister, in her breakdown, completely lost the ability to communicate with other people, than when she heard that the child of a female family member (whom she had never seen) had crashed his bicycle and broken a leg.

When the key was in the lock, she put her hands to her heart, as if she were awaiting some message about the death of a close relative. Oh, dear God, she mumbled, skipping out with quick, tiny steps, tilting from side to side on her short legs, to the kitchen to turn off the tea kettle, which had been put on the gas an hour before and was almost boiled dry. The kitchen was full of steam. Moaning quietly to herself as if there were a fire, she hitched up her dress and crawled up onto a kitchen chair, then stretched the broom handle over the counter to push open the window, even though she knew she couldn't reach to hook the window latch, and she had already broken several panes this way –

He followed her into the dim room awaiting them, and her clear, cool eyes whisked away any creepiness or melancholy. Old junk, they noted, apart from a pretty olive-green corner sofa and a finely carved sewing table. God knows if she would part with any of it if we get married, she thought. What does an old woman like her need all this furniture for?

Suddenly his mother was on her like a cold draft. With embarrassing cordiality she pulled her down and gave her a damp kiss on both cheeks. 'Hello and welcome. I hope you will make yourself at home.' But her voice was plaintive and sad, as if she already foresaw that this person would not only be miserable in the subsequent hours, but that her visit could even cause new problems of unpredictable consequence.

The young woman, who otherwise was rarely embarrassed, felt immediately awkward as she stood there towering over the little old woman, whose brown gaze crept slowly up her youthful form from below, like a wingless insect, slightly diminishing her youthfulness as it made its way up, until the two pairs of eyes met, giving the young woman a vague, overwhelming feeling of anxiety, while a strange attempt at a smile dissolved the mother's heavy, changeable expression. 'Yes, yes,' she sighed. 'It's probably best we use the familiar form of address. Sit right down and I'll make us a cup of tea' (even though we doubtless will die first, before we get that far).

Asger nodded encouragingly to her as she sat down on the piano bench with her back to the piano. He sat in the rocking chair by the window. That old woman was his mother; she had nursed him once. She had actually been young, though this was impossible to imagine. He had blue eyes, there was always a smile quivering around the corners of his mouth, and she loved him. He wasn't at all like that sad, old woman, not at all. He had crawled on this furniture when he was a child. He saw the things here in a totally different way than she did. Naturally. On the wall between the windows hung a painting of him as a child. She pointed at it.

'You were such a cute boy.'

'I look like my father,' he said, glancing at the flower-encircled portrait over the desk. 'Don't you think?'

She got up and went to examine the man's bright, friendly eyes, which put her in a good mood again, because it was quite true that he resembled his father. She walked over to Asger and ran her fingers through his thick brown hair. It was hard for her to keep away from him for very long.

'Is your mother always so – so sad?' she asked carefully.

He thought about it. Then he said, by way of explanation:

'She's from another era. You have to realize she could almost be my grandmother. My oldest brother is nearly fifty.'

He laughed and nodded toward his father's portrait:

'There was life in the old man,' he said.

She laughed too, and looked at her watch. The sun was out. Right outside. It seemed as if its rays reached the windows with the best of intentions, but then had to give up, slide down the wall in vain, and return to space. But maybe the sun came through in the mornings.

The child of an old man, it occurred to her, as she remembered a phrase from some poem: *born of tired loins*. Her own thought shocked her so much she was compelled to go and kneel in front of him, put his head in her hands, and observe his beautiful mouth and his tired eyes with the distant look in them, and his slim hands which could never be still, so were constantly fumbling with a pipe or cigarettes or searching for tobacco or change in all his pockets. He was so forgetful, a bit hesitant in his manner, like a person who never has all his senses in the same place where he actually is.

He didn't kiss her. He glanced nervously at the door.

'Watch out,' he said quickly. 'Here she comes.'

He jumped up and took the tray from his mother. It was so big and heavy, it was a wonder she had gotten that far with it.

The young woman got up too, blushing slightly, and started setting out the cups, while his mother sat down, recovering from the exertion.

'Asger,' she whined, 'would you mind attaching the hook in the kitchen window for me?'

As he left the room, it was evident from his back that he felt he was being watched, and she felt a sudden tenderness arise within her over his charming awkwardness, his dreamy, idealistic view of life, and his amazing ability to feel joy over the most insignificant things; also the wrinkles around his eyes when he smiled, which he evidently got from his father, since his mother didn't seem able to smile – I mean, had she ever laughed in her whole life?

She smiled uncomfortably at the old woman, who nodded slowly and sadly back at her: 'Well, we have to hope it will lead to a blessing this time,' she intoned.

'Yes,' said the young woman quietly, and a shadow passed through her impressionable mind. A reflection from the eyes across from her, so filled with misery, reached her own open and questioning gaze, and a speck of invisible dust settled on her features, as if for a moment she had merged with the silent horde of photographs which spent their shadowy lives here on the furniture and the windowsills, where no flowers seemed to thrive.

His mother poured the tea when Asger returned. She had

dirty fingernails, just like him. But with him it was from all that fidgeting with his pipe, or maybe forgetfulness – at any rate, it didn't matter. But an old woman, she thought, should at least keep herself clean.

The three of them sat around the large round table, so far from one another they had to rise in order to reach the plate of cookies or the fine blue sugar bowl. The young woman's bare summer legs were cold, and appeared pale next to the old woman's dark gypsy-brown skin. Asger took two sugars, and kept stirring his cup long after they had dissolved. It was necessary to say something to him several times before he turned his gaze from the distant point it dwelled on, and looked straight at the person who spoke to him. 'Sorry, what did you ask?' She tended to find this endearing, and she jokingly waved her hand back and forth in front of him, like a person does to see if the other is conscious or not; but even that wasn't always enough to bring him back. Back from what?

He was bored visiting his mother. Naturally. It was morose. She reported on her recent calamities with a dark, droning voice: the little girl who had fallen down the kitchen stairs the other day, and her sister, who was no longer able to communicate. 'But she's not insane, because it's obvious she recognizes me; still, being in such a horrible place must make her feel even more miserable!'

Asger smiled gently.

'Aunt Agnes has always been a bit strange,' he said.

He showed a good appetite, while the young woman sat agonizing over her tea. She felt nauseous. This happened to her sometimes, from hospital smells, for example. She asked Asger for a cigarette and sucked the smoke eagerly into her lungs as if it were fresh air.

'Oh, you smoke too,' said his mother, horrified, and suddenly the young woman looked at her with hardened eyes and thought: You are not going to take him away from me – feeling surprised at herself, because of course there was nothing in the world that could prevent her from loving Asger or that would turn his heart away from her.

The photographs stared into the room. Yellowed, half-faded men with high collars and full beards, and modern, artistic child portraits with embellished chiaroscuro effects. Dark and light eyes, serious and smiling faces, some with the same brooding, heavy expression as Asger's mother, others with hollow, expressionless eyes, as if they were observing the furniture they had once touched and sat on, from somewhere on the other side of the grave. Soon she would be among them, know them, and consort with them. And her children would belong to this heritage for all time and resemble them in some way.

His mother rose and started introducing the family, the dead as well as the living. On the beautiful sewing table were her three daughters-in-law, smiling, slightly apart from the others, as if they were shying away from the rest of the dusty crowd. One had a good-natured, round face with glasses. They probably came to visit often on Sunday with the sons and their children. They knew the round table and the old woman's kisses and moans; maybe they even laughed at her, remembering the first time they were here, when she had terrified them, young and in love as they were. Space could probably be made on the sewing table for another photograph, and on the piano for a couple of grandchildren.

Asger sat in the rocking chair filling his pipe, while his mother bustled about, presenting the pictures. He was probably impatiently waiting to leave, but controlling himself, as one does with parents. 'I'm her last one, you know,' he had said, 'so she still thinks of me as a child.'

'And then here is Aunt Agnete, who died last year. She suffered so much at the end – and here is my eldest son; he's a doctor in Holstebro.' The doctor had an ill-defined, limp mouth, and eyes so pale that in the picture they seemed to have no expression. Did he look like his mother or his father? The next one, a teacher in a community college, definitely resembled the mother, but in a refined, melancholy, weary way. The brown eyes stared out questioningly at the young woman.

'He doesn't look like Asger,' she said, unbelievably happy that he didn't; she wasn't sure why.

She peered over at the man she loved. He was sitting with his ankles crossed on top of the table with the photos of his three sisters-in-law, and he was reading the newspaper, from behind which blue pipe smoke rose. His chin came to a sharp point before merging into his neck – a sign of character and steadfastness. Yes, his chin did do that –

The gallery was endless. Outside the sun was shining. She was going to suggest to Asger that they go for a walk in the woods afterward, then they could lie on his jacket and look up into the fine, bright greenery until the late twilight coolness forced them closer, and he would warm her with his healthy young body and rid her of her strange anxiousness, and promise he would never take her to visit his mother again, or, at any rate, only on birthdays and similar occasions, when other people were there too. Actually, he could come over and help her out a little, instead of just retreating and sitting there. Suddenly she felt irritated at how he always made himself comfortable wherever he went, not because he enjoyed being there, but because of something else in his personality, something no one could penetrate, and which was always with him. At first she had thought it was only when he was with her that he had trouble pulling himself away, but even when they went to the movies it was a struggle for him to get up and leave when the film ended. He was aware of it. He said it was a kind of inertia.

'And here is Aunt Agnes, whom I mentioned before. This was taken just before she was admitted for the first time.'

The young woman glanced from the mother to the picture and quickly back again. She didn't see any difference.

'She looks so much like you,' she exclaimed.

The old woman nodded solemnly.

'We do resemble one another quite a bit now, both in mind and body, but that hasn't always been the case.'

She tottered over to the desk and fished out of a drawer an old faded photograph of a young girl, a very pretty young girl with a blond top knot and a narrow velvet band around her bare neck. Her forehead was high and broad, her eyes brown and slightly slanted, her mouth on the verge of a secretive smile.

'This is Agnes at twenty-two.'

The young woman hesitantly took the picture in her hand and stared at it. Then she said into the air:

'Incredible how she looks like – I mean, there is such a resemblance to –'

Then a sudden chill crept up from her legs, and both women glanced over at Asger, who was cleaning his pipe, oblivious to their attention and conversation. The old woman nodded. 'I know, there's something around the mouth,' she said, vaguely triumphant, or maybe just with the kind of satisfaction all parents feel upon seeing their own features replicated in their children. She looked intently at the young

woman and repeated, slightly louder: 'There really is a strik-
ing resemblance around the mouth.'

And his beloved couldn't understand it, and didn't know
why it was so unsettling. She didn't even know if that was
the cause, or if it would still affect her when she had left
the room and its atmosphere, but an anxiety she had never
before experienced in her life wrapped unmercifully around
her like a cloak, when she admitted that the young woman in
the picture – the one who later went crazy – had a small, weak
mouth with tiny smile wrinkles continuing out to her cheeks,
just like Asger.

He took a deep breath when they were out on the street.

'So, was it bad?' he asked, tenderly teasing, and adding,
when she didn't respond, 'We had to get it over with – so
what do you want to do now? Is it too late to go to the woods?'

He was in a great mood. He had gotten through something unpleasant. But the young woman looked askance at
him with tears in her eyes for that mouth she had loved, which
was now ruined for her. So far, just that.

Then she said, 'You know what, I'm kind of tired. I think
I would rather go home.' And she had to hurry home to be
alone, before the tears really started flowing – tears over something that maybe wasn't completely broken, but would still
never be the same.

Up above, from behind the curtains, his mother stood
watching them, motionless and unseen, her eyes dark and
imbued with emotion. In her hand she was still holding the
picture of her sick sister.

Queen of the Night

While her mother powdered her face and pulled the white angel-hair wig down over her forehead, Grete held up the mirror for her.

Grete was kneeling on a chair, leaning in over the table from the other side, staring from behind the mirror with open mouth and wide eyes, round and shiny with excitement.

'That looks so great,' she said.

Her mother whispered nervously, 'Ssh, you'll wake Daddy.' She wrinkled her forehead while applying a thick, greasy pencil to her eyebrows. Then she turned her head and peeked in the mirror to see how far into her temples the line should go. Her skin looked brown as coffee against the white wig. Grete put out her hand.

'Can I touch it?' she whispered.

'Hold the mirror up for me.'

Grete pulled back her hand.

'Oww,' she said, surprised.

The white artificial hair hurt her fingertips.

Her father stirred on the sofa behind her, and both of them went stiff until he settled down again.

Grete sat up on the table, because it made her belly hurt to hang over the edge. Next to her lay an orange lipstick, to go with the white hair, and a little case with black eyeshadow, which was wet in the middle from spit. Black and red and white and silver. Her mother's costume made a nice crinkling sound when she moved, and she smelled nice too. Her father lay there sleeping behind her. He had to work a night shift, and her mother had to make sure to be home early in the morning before he got off work. Karneval festivities might last all night, but a man could never understand that. Men didn't go to Karneval. There were some pictures of men in the magazine where her mother had found the pattern for her costume, but they just looked foolish. Men went to work, and when they were home they slept. Karneval was for ladies.

Grete was glad she wasn't a boy.

Finally she was able to put down the heavy mirror and admire her mother, who was standing in front of the sideboard, holding up the black tarlatan gown with both hands to see if the skirt could be taken off over her head. Grete blushed at how pretty her mother looked. Nothing on her neck or shoulders, and the rest a profusion of eleven yards of billowing tarlatan at one krone per yard (but to her father they said it cost half) with glimmering silver sequins strewn all over. Every single one was sewn on by hand, and they glistened in the light from the bare bulb in the ceiling when she turned – slow and rustling, fragrant and unreal in the modest living room.

She smiled at her daughter, careful not to wrinkle her makeup.

'Do I look fine?' she asked.

Grete nodded eagerly.

The costume was called 'Queen of the Night'. It was the nicest one in the whole magazine. Last year her mother was

'Coachman from the 1800s' in blue and gold satin with a high, black, cardboard hat and boy's knee pants. The cloth for that one had only cost two kroner, but her father, as usual, still had to calculate how many bags of oatmeal or pounds of carrots could have been bought with the money. What nonsense. They had oatmeal and carrots to eat anyway, and her mother didn't get many chances to enjoy herself, and it wasn't her fault he was unemployed half the year, so she had to go out and clean for other people.

Grete was completely convinced they would be better off if her father wasn't around, because he was the only one who put her mother in a bad mood – apart from when the other wives in the building gossiped about her. They were quick to judge. Her mother said they were jealous because she was still youthful and wasn't going to give up every pleasure just because she had a husband who didn't like to dance. When Grete turned fourteen, her mother would take her to Karneval. That was in four more years. Then she would be 'Queen of the Night', with a beauty mark on her cheek and white silken hair. And maybe a black fan. Grete had been up and down the whole street to find one, but the Karneval stores only had colored fans left. In the magazine it said the fan was meant for 'Carmen', but her mother liked it when there were accessories to her costume. Tonight she would have to be satisfied with a little black silken bag she had gotten from a place she had worked, and then of course the half-mask with the fringes over the mouth.

Her father opened his eyes. He hadn't actually been sleeping at all, because he usually awoke very noisily. They noticed him lying there watching them, and her mother's smile disappeared while Grete sat down and started rotating a toy ring around her finger. Her heart was hammering in her chest.

'Look at you,' he said with a gravelly voice. 'You look like a

Christmas decoration. People are going to make fun of you, you old scarecrow.'

Grete's back hurt, as if someone had hit her. Her vision went blurry with hate for her father. She pressed the ring's metal setting into her index finger, which made a white mark that slowly turned red. She didn't dare move, afraid that her mother wouldn't make it out the door in one piece. She heard her mother's breathing behind her.

Her father sat down on the edge of the sofa and felt for his slippers underneath it with his feet. There was crud on his face in the two wrinkles that went from his nose to his mouth. He didn't take his eyes off her mother.

'You should go to work like that tomorrow,' he said mockingly. 'You might be able to take a taxi there, if you can find someone crazy enough to pay for it.'

Her mother didn't answer. Grete heard her go out to the entry and put on her jacket. The mask was still lying on the table, but Grete didn't dare bring it to her, for fear of drawing her father's attention. If only he could fall down from some scaffolding and die – or drown – in a marl pit – then everything would be fine.

Tears dripped down on the bare, stained tabletop. Grete bit her knuckles and tried to think about Karneval. About the 'Queen of the Night' in a flood of lights and with all the other cupids and dancers and Carmens like graceful shadows around her. A shiny parquet floor and the melancholy quivering of violins. The 'Queen of the Night' glides dreamily across the floor with a soft, faraway look in her eyes. Sequins like moonlight sprinkle in her wake. She takes Grete by the hand and leads her into the light –

The front door slammed shut, and quick steps retreated down the stairs.

Grete cautiously turned her head to see her father sitting on the sofa staring vacantly into the room. She stood up and started to clean up after her mother. There wasn't anything to be afraid of anymore. There never was when she was alone with her father. Sometimes he tried to entertain her a little, but of course he knew nothing about dresses, lipstick, or dancing. He wanted her to read Grimm's *Fairy Tales*, but they were too boring and only for little kids. She liked the novel series in *Family Journal* a lot better. It was about a young girl who didn't know if the young men were attracted to her for her money. And then one of them apparently put poison in her food, but that would be explained in the next issue. Her mother read it too. It was completely different from reading about fairies and trolls, which didn't even exist!

In the shelter of the mirror, Grete let the orange-colored lipstick glide over her lips, and she lifted her eyebrows and smiled coyly at her reflection, with her head at a slight angle. She teased out her hair, wondering how it would look if she got a perm. Her mother had promised her one the next first of the month, when she would get a pay rise, but her father mustn't know about it. She put her hand over her mouth and giggled at the thought. Then she cast a sidelong glance at her father. He was still sitting in the same position, bent forward with his big hands clasped together as if he were greeting himself.

Grete got up from the chair and walked over to him.

'Daddy,' she said hesitantly.

He looked at her. Strangely. Almost as if he couldn't remember who she was. His eyes were kind of sad. But he could just stop being so mean to her mother. And not say that she was an old scarecrow!

Her heart felt tight because of his eyes. She turned away

and started collecting pieces of cloth and sequins from the floor. She picked up one of them. It was just a piece of bent metal.

Her father stood up and looked at the clock. He cleared his throat.

'Well, I guess I've got to get going,' he said in a completely normal voice, and Grete breathed a bit easier, regretting the marl pit. But why did he always scare them so much? You couldn't ask him about anything or talk with him the same way as her mother, who told Grete everything.

He started putting on his boots.

'Aren't you afraid to sleep alone?' he asked, with the strange, shy voice he used when he was trying to be nice to her, even though he was mad at her mother.

Grete pushed her hair back and smiled bravely at him. She was still a *little* scared, even though it was silly to feel that way.

'No,' she said intrepidly. 'When you're asleep, you can't be afraid.'

Her father laughed hoarsely, and something bright arose inside Grete: Just imagine if he could always be nice and in a good mood.

Then he put his packed sandwich in his pocket and awkwardly stroked the girl's hair.

'What do you want to be when you grow up?' he asked.

'Queen of the Night,' she shouted with excitement, but bowed her head as if from a blow when she saw her father's expression change. But he didn't hit her; he just turned away and walked out the door without saying goodbye.

She stood there, staring in confusion at the closed door. Then she felt cold, and went and peeked in the lukewarm stove. There was a pile of ashes in front of it from the morning. She should probably go to bed, but there was still straightening up to do. Why did her father get angry so suddenly? Hopefully her mother would come home soon.

She bent down and pushed the costume scraps into a pile with one hand. She could get a broom from the kitchen and sweep them up, but she never liked making a noise when she was home alone. She added the pile to the ashes, then she crouched down and looked at it. She reached out her hand, picked up a curl that had been cut off the wig, and pressed it between her fingers. It stung like nettle but she grasped it even tighter.

This must be made of glass, she thought, feeling something warm running down her cheeks. It was silly to cry over something like that.

She knew beforehand it would hurt.

One Morning in a Residential Neighborhood

It was fall, but the little girl insisted it was winter because she was cold, and she was wearing her new brown winter coat for the first time. Early that morning she had been woken by Hansen, even though her older brother was still sleeping. There was something unusual and exciting in the air, but she was so sleepy, she couldn't remember just then what was in store for her.

Hansen's voice was strangely slurred, and she was caressing every piece of clothing as if it were alive before she put it on the girl. The girl became attentive and took a closer look at the person she had known her entire short life. 'Why are you crying?' she asked, surprised. But that made Hansen upset, and she mumbled something about having a cold, that's why her eyes were red. She hadn't been crying.

Suddenly the girl realized what day it was, and her round little face broke out in a smile and she started babbling, 'I'm going on a trip with Daddy, Hansen, you know that, right? Can I say goodbye to Ole? Are Mommy and Daddy up yet?' But Hansen just shushed her and gently reprimanded her, saying, 'Don't wake up Ole; Daddy is up, but Mommy is still asleep.'

Then she led the girl from the dark, warm nursery, where the air was sweet and thick with the sleep of little children.

The girl was wearing her birthday dress, and she wanted to see herself in the mirror. Her nanny lifted her up. 'There you go; you're the one who gets to go with Daddy,' she said. 'You can bet Ole is upset he's not going.' Out of the flat, shiny mirror, two curious, excited eyes stared out at the child's own, but behind them was an adult's damp, pale face, and the child suddenly threw her arms around her nanny's neck. 'When am I coming back home?' she asked. There was a sudden touch of anxiousness in her voice. Hansen didn't answer, but set her carefully back down on the floor and started brushing the girl's long blonde hair with a slightly trembling hand. A little later she was able to say, 'It won't be so very long,' in a voice that she thought would be reassuring. Then she remembered the mother's numerous house rules. One of them was: You always have to tell a child the truth. She would rather be skinned alive than tell the truth at that moment. A wave of anger swept through her toward the mother of the child she loved more than any of the children she had ever known before in her life. They share children between them as if they were furniture, she thought, and when she heard the father's heavy steps upstairs: That poor man; she is destroying his world right now. She forgot about her self-effacing tenderness for the wife when she was sick and the children had to be kept away from her; and when she was healthy and sang during her morning shower, carefree and youthful; and the *thing* behind all of it. That kind of person, she thought vaguely, but got no further, before sorrow ambushed her again. Her tears dropped soundlessly into the girl's hair, glowing like a radiant halo around her precious little face.

The father came down the stairs, and she could see right

away that he hadn't had enough sleep. He had dark circles under his eyes, and the young nanny didn't dare meet his gaze. She walked out to the kitchen to make coffee, and the child ran to her father, who picked her up in his arms and tried to smile. 'So, Kirsten, are you going on a trip with Daddy?' She was like a living ball of joy as she jumped down, then started running up the stairs, because everything wouldn't be so wonderful if her Mommy wasn't part of it. Her father tried to stop her, saying quietly, just like Hansen, 'Mommy is still sleeping.' He stood at the base of the stairs, combing his fingers through his hair, perplexed, while the child ran into her mother's bedroom, where it smelled soothingly of perfume, night, and mother. When she crawled in next to the warm, comforting body, her face got wet, and the delicate, vague anxiety returned for a moment. She said, 'Why are you crying, Mommy? I'll come back.' Her mother didn't answer, but pulled the little girl closer. They lay together like that, silently: the child confused and impatient, and the mother so distraught by grief and shame that her entire body was trembling like a sapling in a storm. Trembling, but motionless. Between her and the child was an invisible being, an unmerciful power. In a few hours, two strong arms would substitute for the child's tender, pure embrace. A lover's voice would comfort and explain. The fine autumn air in the yard, the flowers' aroma, and the long, happy days would temper the loss, and she knew it, and it made her feel weak and fallible: Dear God, she prayed, let this parting be the last one in my life.

The jumpy little body wriggled itself from her arms. The child wanted to envelop her with her happiness, and she tried to pull her mother out of bed, as she had done so many times before, so everything would be okay. 'Get up now, Mommy,'

she shouted. 'You have to see the moving van. You have to
wave goodbye to us. I'm going to put on my new coat – it's
winter, Mommy. Do you remember when it was winter, and
you went sledding with me and Daddy and Ole?'

She stayed upstairs while her mother dressed. The aroma
of coffee rose to the bedroom, and with it a restlessness. The
girl's brother was awake. Soon he would come running to
say good morning, and probably be crabby because he wasn't
going with his daddy. Daddy had found work in another city!
Children are so willing to be tricked to avoid the truth they
don't want to hear.

The little girl remained standing there mercilessly, while
her mother did her hair at the vanity. Soon the movers would
come tramping in, and carry down the furniture he wanted
to take. She had begged him to take everything, to stay in the
house and chase her out, if only she could keep both children.
Fathers always forget their children when they haven't seen
them for a long time. But what did she really know about that?
If she had been more confident, she could have invoked the
law, which rarely separates a child from its mother. But she
wasn't certain about anything anymore, and she wasn't used
to making big decisions on her own. Two different men
wanted her to make this sacrifice. 'You can't take everything
from him.' She owed it to two men. But a person doesn't
sacrifice a child, do they? Well, she was doing it. Only her. It
was her fault, and the most innocent of all people would pay
for it. Here in this room, with the child beside her, she felt
completely alone. Even the furniture seemed to shrink from
her. Everything she knew was receding into a fog. If only it
all could go back to how it was before! But nothing is ever
the way it was. Life is change: passion, indifference, death.
She was afraid of her child, afraid of all the life awaiting her

downstairs: Miss Hansen's tearful, shaming, uncomprehending eyes; Ole's questions; and her husband's pained face. Oh God, this child! If only she had been a bit younger or a bit older. The people we love, she thought, as she put makeup on her pale face. What can I say? How can I stop it? My love, come and help me. Maybe it's too late for you to come. The pain of this morning will always be mine and mine alone. You will feel jealous if I even mention it. But all of us are alone. We three adults have been living here together in this house all these years. We love the children and they love us, and now we have to lie to them. How can I live a virtuous life when the footsteps and voice of a man can turn my heart away from everything that once gave me comfort? Why did I get married? Why did I have children? There is nothing so merciless as love.

Her eyes met the child's observant ones in the mirror, and she smiled at her. The girl jumped up on her mother's lap and put her warm cheek against her mother's. 'Mommy, today you have to eat breakfast with us, okay?' she said ingratiatingly, using the fine little voice she used – the one she had used quite often lately – when she wanted to chase away unpleasantness between the grown-ups.

Carrying her daughter she went downstairs, where the table was set for all of them. Otherwise the children usually ate by themselves. Her husband sat in his usual spot, and she immediately made the same observation as the nanny: He didn't sleep last night! She felt bad for him, as we do for people we have harmed. He sat there with his grief and hurt wrapped around him like a frayed jacket for everyone to see and feel sorry for. And here I come with my sacrifice, she thought; and to bear it, she had to imagine the face of her lover in front of her like an invisible shield. But the three pairs of eyes, which were turned mutely toward her, made her waver. She despised

herself: Is all of life like an opera? She wanted to sing: Goodbye, goodbye, now I'm leaving and I'm taking someone else
instead of you.

She sat down, defiant and erect at the table end, smiling bravely at her children. But she didn't dare look at Miss
Hansen. Why did she arrange this comical farce, she thought
angrily. All that's missing is lit candles on the table. Her son
was grumpy and sleepy, as she had predicted. Suddenly she
gave him an icy look, as if he had nothing to do with her,
while she pushed in the chair under her daughter and tied
the bib around her neck. For a moment it all seemed to her
like a long, drawn-out sentimental scene from an American
film, constructed so pitifully that people react by bursting out
laughing: The sweet children, the wronged father, the loyal
maid, and the flighty mother. What did all these people have
to do with her? Why were they taking advantage of her love
for this child? Only one single person really mattered to her,
and he wasn't here. But his shadow suffused her expression
like a flimsy defense against something horrible. And beyond
him: millions of miserable children, tons of loyal housekeepers and an incalculable army of lovers, abandoned husbands,
disloyal husbands, betrayed and flighty women, all kinds of
people, all kinds of lives, and all equally lonely. And overshad-
owing everything: some kind of law, war, profound misery,
making a living, fear of the newspapers' bold headlines, a
world in tension, and hopelessly patient calm. A whip is raised
over all of us; where and whom will it hit?

She ate her egg in silence, letting the nanny take care of the
children. She still had not met her husband's gaze. You have
to do it, her lover had said. Time is of the essence. If you keep
on being weak and yielding, life will pass you by. Try to see it
from a broader perspective.

But soon the moving van would be there, and it was up to them to make it a celebratory event for the girl. They had agreed on that. She pulled herself together and was about to say something, when Ole, who was going to turn eight soon, suddenly looked around strangely from one to the other and asked, 'So when is Kirsten coming back home?'

No one was able to answer. As soon as the girl was out of the house, she would have to explain to him how things were. He was old enough to understand, and it was important that he also believed something new and exciting was in store for him.

All at once she felt so terribly tired, hating the nanny, who sniffled loudly, hating all of them because they didn't understand her, and hating herself most of all because she didn't know if she was doing the right thing. She felt a sudden, crushing desire to sob in her lover's arms. Her tears were stuck, burning behind her dry eyes. How did a five-year-old child comprehend this? When would she feel betrayed, and how would the truth come out?

Finally the moving van arrived, red and boisterous and festive, and the children ran out to the road to catch sight of the men who would carry so much away. The nanny got up and ran to her room, and the two of them were alone for a moment. They had nothing to say to one another, but a strange feeling of mutual pain was in their eyes when they eventually met. He blinked a few times like a young boy, and she saw something in his expression that she had once loved.

It wasn't possible for him to hate her. For some reason he had become used to not blaming her for her actions. He was indifferent about his own life; he was only consumed with the thought that he didn't want to die. A person doesn't die when he has a child to take care of and protect. Besides, she could see the girl once in a while, if she wanted to, and he wanted to see his son. But at this moment he felt the same mild indifference for himself that she did. It was as if they only had this one child together. He had fertilized her back then, and now he was taking the child with him. She had to pay. But she would forget soon enough. When a woman is in love –

For twenty minutes there was noise and activity throughout the house, and then the girl was sitting next to the driver in her fine brown coat with a velvet cap over her blonde curls. She looked at her mother with a slightly anxious expression, and she put her arms around her one last time and whispered to comfort her, 'When it's summer I'll come back, okay?'

Her mother nodded and smiled and waved, as long as she could see the van. Then the smile faded from her face, as if a hard hand had wiped it off. She took the boy by the hand and started walking slowly back to the house.

A Nice Boy

The forest warden's son squeezed between the other customers in the bakery shop. He stood on his toes to be seen, and he kept a close eye on who came in after him. He was in a hurry. He almost always was. He needed a bottle of milk for his little brother. His mother was suddenly unable to nurse him anymore, because she had a tumor in her breast, and a fever.

He craned his neck trying to catch the eye of the baker, who was really taking his time. The mother of one of his classmates came into the store, and he quickly removed his hat, like a recruit to an officer. 'Hello,' he said.

She was grappling with a shopping bag in front of her, from which the ends of leeks stuck out and tickled his neck.

'Hello, John. Congratulations on your new little brother. Isn't it wonderful?'

'Yep,' he said, blushing bright red in his effort to express overwhelming joy.

They all turned to stare at him. Was he really happy?

'No one was expecting that, were they?' said the baker, smiling at a customer. 'Got it in just under the wire.'

Then he turned to the boy.

'And what do you need today?'

John lifted his basket up onto the counter and handed him the note his mother had written. 'Otherwise you'll forget half of it,' she had said. He had never forgotten anything yet, but she always said things like that. He took the filled basket from the baker, with the change wrapped in the note.

'Is he a cute little one?' asked the baker, stroking his beard.

The boy nodded. 'I guess,' he said, 'but he screams a lot.'

They all laughed, like adults always do when you don't just say 'yes' or 'no'. He thought he saw them looking at one another and winking as he hurried out the door.

Outside, the cold greeted him and made him sneeze. The woods rose like a huge mountain in front of him, and the house at the bottom was like a tiny dot. If he ran across the fields, he could be home in fifteen minutes; on the road it took half an hour. But it was too light out to trespass.

The basket was heavy, so he switched it to his other arm and continued at a half-run. He wanted to surprise his mother by coming back lightning-fast, which he always did. But today he wanted it to be even faster, because she was sick and his little brother needed the milk right away. Cars streamed past him, but he couldn't see the license plates, which he otherwise kept track of, because of the snowflakes. A few cyclists struggled by, bent over their handlebars, with earmuffs and damp, red faces. But the ones coming toward him had the wind at their backs, and he recognized all of them. 'Hi John!' they shouted. He nodded enthusiastically. No one could say he was impolite. He was the nicest boy in the whole area when it came to running errands, chopping wood, washing diapers, and whatever else a person has to do to get ahead in the world. The only thing that didn't go so smoothly was his schoolwork. His mother said, 'Don't worry about that; as long as you're a nice boy.' His mother was so sweet, and so kind. He was a little scared of his father, who didn't talk to him very much. His father's voice was coarse and hard, just like his hands when he slung the rifle down from his shoulder and tossed a dead squirrel on the kitchen counter. They were harmful animals, and he got money from the estate owner for every one he shot. But they looked comical when they dashed up the tree trunks, always running away. John wished he could hold a live squirrel in his hands one day. They wouldn't have to be scared of him. He had only touched his father's rifle once, and he still remembered the spanking he got for it. 'It could go off,' his mother had explained, 'and hit you or one of us.' What if it hit his little brother? Who knows what would happen? Then his mother and father would regret ever 'taking him in'.

He raced ahead at the thought. He knew he was in debt to humanity because he wasn't born properly to his mother and father like his little brother, but had ended up with them, by an improbable stroke of luck. He was adopted, and his real parents were horrible people from Copenhagen, who weren't even married. 'God forbid you ever meet them,' his mother had said when she told him that. For a while afterward he would stare at the outsiders who visited his town, imagining they had come from Copenhagen to take him away. He would put up such a fight and yell for his mother! He might be small for a seven year old, but he was strong. He could pump water from the well and carry two buckets at once. Little brother might never be able to do that. Such a runt. He lay at his mother's breast, sucking like crazy until it made her sick. One day John asked if *he* had ever eaten like that, and his mother laughed. 'No, you poor thing; you were bottle-fed.' He imagined that he might have been made in a bottle, just like people make ships in bottles, but now he knew what it meant. It just sounded so strange to be different. And he would always be different, but only in a good way. He could run faster than any boy in his class.

His breath steamed from his mouth like smoke from his father's pipe. He sniffled and switched the basket between his arms again. Then he paused to wipe his nose on his sleeve. Now the woods weren't like a mountain anymore, and he could see smoke rising from the chimney. He could also hear an axe chopping, which was his father, felling trees. The estate owner marked the victims himself. They just stood there not knowing anything until they felt the axe on their trunks. Until then, they were just like any other trees, figuring they would stand there for all time, blowing in the wind, sending out new shoots in the spring and losing it all when the cold arrived, making the poor squirrels visible from a distance. He felt bad for the trees, but his mother said trees didn't feel anything. The little squirrels didn't know they had to be shot either, and it didn't hurt them at all when their heart was struck by a pellet. Only poachers were bad, because they often didn't shoot right, and they let the animals lie there until his father found them. His father loved animals. They had three hunting dogs and a little fox terrier, which was going to be shot soon, because it shed, and all the dog hair made little brother cough. The doctor had said that. Still, John loved that dog.

The arrival of the baby had brought with it lots of other things. In the middle of the night the baby woke him with his screaming, and even when John broke his own record crossing the distance from the bakery or from school, sometimes his mother forgot to notice. In his disappointment he pointed it out to her himself. 'I made it in only ten minutes today, Mommy –' and she looked briefly in his direction and exclaimed, 'You are incredible. You are the best ever. What would we ever do without you?' But it wasn't as big a deal as it used to be.

Without thinking about it, the boy slowed down in the final stretch. The milk was sloshing in the bottle. 'It is amazing how much the little tyke can get down,' said his mother, with the baby at her bosom. But in a different tone of voice than when they said (and it was mostly his father): 'The way he puts it away he'll eat us out of house and home.' Then it was John they meant. And the food caught in his throat, while his cheeks turned bright red. Then his mother laughed and patted his head. 'If only all that eating would make him taller,' she said kindly. So his father hadn't meant anything mean by it. But still!

He jumped up a snowbank at the road edge, slid down the other side, and looked up at the next one. He laughed at his little game, and forgot he was in a hurry. His mother was home in bed, sick because of the baby, and his father would come home soon from the woods and make dinner, while John set the table. It felt strange to eat alone with him. When he was in a good mood, he teased the boy. 'So Mister Front Teeth,' he said, 'how was your day?' John had lost his two front teeth, and the father insisted they wouldn't grow back. 'That's nonsense,' said his mother, annoyed. 'The boy could go and think it was true!' His dear mother – so fat, so warm, so good.

He started running again for the last little bit, past the pump that looked like an old man with a cold, with clothes draped all over it so it wouldn't freeze; past a load of firewood standing in the farmyard, waiting for its turn in the stove. He had helped to stack it during the summer. He had pretended the pieces of wood were soldiers, and really he wanted to stand them up vertically in ranks, but that took up too much space.

Work was his play and play his work. And that was perfectly fine, until his little brother was born. Then the wet diapers became pirate flags, but he was a tired little pirate who had too many enemies to overcome. And the baby was a prince, who was going to inherit a kingdom one day. John was his slave, whom he always sought for advice in difficult situations. 'Ask my slave,' he would say. 'He brought me up, so he gets to decide everything.'

John lifted the door latch and stepped into the kitchen. Then he put the basket on the stove and stood there listening. There was a voice coming from the living room in addition to his mother's. They didn't hear him come in. He could hear it was their neighbor, Mrs Petersen, who often came by to have a cup of coffee.

'Well, aren't you thrilled that you were finally able to?' To what? It wasn't nice to eavesdrop, but it sounded so interesting.

'Do you really have to ask, after all these years?'

'If only you had known when you took in John!' It sounded like a complaint, and John stiffened at hearing his own name.

'Well,' his mother said hesitantly, 'we've never been sorry about that for a moment. He is such a nice and capable boy.'

'He certainly has been a big help to you.'

There was something about the tone that made a little pain gnaw deep into John.

'Well, Mrs Petersen, it's no trouble for him. He's never happier than when he can help us with something.' Now his mother sounded upset, and John wanted to run in there and support her. But he wanted to hear himself praised a bit more too.

'No, of course,' said the other woman effusively. 'And God knows where the poor child would have been without you. It was such a good deed you did. Is he thankful? Because he knows, doesn't he?'

'He is definitely thankful,' said his mother, and out by the kitchen door John stood thankfully and in solidarity with her. 'And of course we have told him. A child finds out those kinds of things sooner or later, and my husband also thought it was for the best.'

He pulled off his mittens and stopped listening. His heart was pounding. He hadn't run fast enough; he wasn't thankful enough. He wasn't like other children. He was 'taken in'. Inside him, a bad conscience started growing like a heavy, thick substance. He wanted to light the stove before his father got home. He wanted to get the bottle ready for his little brother and make a scrambled egg with sugar for his mother. He wanted to get up tonight when the baby cried, so his mother could stay asleep, he wanted –

'Well, God Almighty, are you standing there, John?'

Mrs Petersen tied her kerchief around her head and stared at him dubiously. Had he heard anything? He wasn't as adorable as the little one in there, she concluded. You never really warm up to children like that, but he did work like a horse all day long while other children were playing. Everyone talked about this and acted as if they found it troubling, but deep inside they all thought it was perfectly fine.

The boy bowed his head, afraid she was going to take his hand. Her hands were so limp and always smelled like dishwater or something else repulsive. They reminded him of the dead animals on the kitchen counter that his father got money for killing – squirrels and voles, and sometimes a small deer with gentle, stiffened eyes and legs sticking out, like it couldn't get over the surprise that suddenly everything was gone forever. To get shot is like falling asleep, his mother said, who used to feel bad for all the little creatures herself.

Mrs Petersen left, and the boy hurried into the living room.

His mother lay on the sofa looking exhausted, with her eyes closed. The baby was sleeping in the cradle by the wood stove.

'Wasn't I fast?' he asked carefully.

Slowly she opened her eyes.

'Oh, it's you,' she said. 'You are such a good boy.' Then she dozed off again. The boy heard the clunk of his father outside, taking off his clogs, and the dogs barking and rushing at the door.

He stood there looking at his mother lying with her mouth open. He wanted to be even better and run even faster. He knew he owed a debt to these people, which he paid off in little installments and with his meager abilities. If only I was big, he thought, growing sleepy from the warmth in the room. Feeling uneasy, he snuck past his father in the little entry and out to the kitchen. His father didn't greet him, perhaps didn't even notice him.

'How is the little one?' he shouted.

'Shhh,' whispered his mother gently. 'He's sleeping.'

Then the boy started to light the stove. The cold iron rings stung like fire against his numbed hands.

Life's Persistence

The waiting room was filled with women who avoided looking at one another. They looked down at the dusty floor, at
the tips of their shoes, at the dirty wall of undefinable color.
(Why is it that these doctors who earn so much money always
have such shabby offices? Maybe he won't even wear a lab
coat and he probably has dirty fingernails.) They were all
so discreet and dressed so self-effacingly, they could slip in
anywhere without anyone noticing them. Maybe they had
received the same advice she had: *He determines the price based
on your clothing.* Besides, the other women were no business
of hers. Couldn't she drop her habit of concerning herself
with everyone and everything around her, just this once? No.
She couldn't bring the seriousness of the situation into focus.
Was it all that serious after all? In any case it wasn't any worse
for her than for the others. Behind each of these women was
the shadow of a man: a tired husband who toiled for a throng
of children, and whose income couldn't bear the strain of
another child; a disloyal chap with pomaded hair who was
already a thing of the past, an ephemeral, hasty tryst that
had little to do with love; a student who was loved but too

young, who was now pacing outside on the sidewalk, teetering between hope and fear; a carefree, superficial guy who had 'found an address' and bought a way out of the predicament he had gotten himself into; or one who had moved away from the city and left his difficult burden here like a piece of forgotten furniture; at any rate a man, a trap, a careless, costly experience, maybe the first one –

There was no rush to get inside the closed door, which every now and then was opened from the inside by a young woman, who, quickly and without looking at anyone, left the sad waiting room, relieved or not, to slip back into the afternoon's noisy rush hour traffic, down below on the other side of the murky windows.

It was so quiet. Alice thought about Bent. There was something clearly laughable about the thought of having a child with him, and not the least heroic in hiding it from him. A child? A little wrinkled thing under powder-blue ruffles, staring out at the world with the unknowing intelligent gaze of an infant. A bond between two who loved one another; but their love couldn't bear a bond like that. They agreed on that from the beginning. He was burdened enough by a wife who let him do whatever he wanted, as long as she and their child were supported and the outer appearance of civility and domesticity was maintained. Why should Alice come and disrupt that calm? She looked at her relationship to Bent with cool reason. He was only loving if she kept it easy and ephemeral. In that way she had extended it to nearly a year, and when they hadn't had any accidents, they had become careless. It was mostly her fault. A person doesn't go around thinking they will break their leg every time they cross the street. And anyway she wasn't going to reproach others for something that happened to her. And if it were the man's body that had to go through this, she knew that Bent would never have complained to her about it, just as he barely complained to her about his marriage tedium, which naturally was not as tedious as the way he expressed it to her, albeit tactfully. When he came home from work, their child jumped up to greet him, and he picked it up in his arms and they played together. Then he kissed his wife and was happy about her pretty, domestic appearance, the finely set table, the aromas emanating from the kitchen, and his desk, which alone bore the mark of his disorganized habits and his quick-witted mind with its clear, cool, reasoning intellect, which she loved about him. But all of this was conjecture on her part. He never talked about it, and she wasn't curious. She abhorred the usual: My wife doesn't understand me, etc. She had patiently shared him with this strange woman whom she had never seen. Don't demand much, and you'll get more. And if she just caressed his forehead, the memory of his life apart from hers was gone for several hours. This is how she held onto his love, and he didn't harm either of them. *Neither of us,* she stated clearly in her mind. For some reason it was important to recognize that.

She turned her gaze somewhat uneasily toward the closed door and felt a little dispirited. A distasteful undertaking, she thought. Nothing to do with murder or 'the sanctity of motherhood' – phrases she had had plenty of from the proper law-abiding doctors in proper lab coats behind proper desks. She was twenty-five years old and master of her own body, not according to the law, which she could not care less about, but because she *wanted* to be. Not a single sentimental thought about powder-blue ruffles and a little toothless grin. There were already plenty of babies in the world. And this little parasite had only brought her nausea and discomfort, and left a slimy, gray veil over everything that used to be nice: the first rays of morning under the roll-down shades; the coffee she had to switch to tea, which didn't taste good to her anymore either; the evening's heart-wrenching yearning for Bent, which had changed into yawning exhaustion, difficult to keep hidden for long. Besides, recently he had only come by a couple of times a week. That made sense. She wasn't too crazy about being with a man who just wanted to feel good and fall asleep in her arms. She remembered how agitated she was when he had a tooth abscess which made his cheek swell up, and they couldn't be seen out together. It fit as badly with his handsome, well-chiseled face as a grotesque swollen belly would fit with her hourglass waist, of which she was so proud. Everything oppressive about marriage had to be kept out of their relationship. Wouldn't it look fine if she called him up now and said in a tearful wifely voice: There's something we absolutely have to discuss right now! She wasn't the strongest person, for better or for worse. She wasn't going to try to convince him to leave his wife and child on account of this accident. She was afraid of hurting anyone, and she had the innate conviction that love and marriage rarely had anything to do with one another.

Her turn was approaching soon; in her mind she repeated her false name and her 'desperate circumstances'. He would ask, 'Why can't you keep the baby?', spuriously and pro forma. She already couldn't stand him, the way you might feel antipathy toward a stranger on whose mercy you depend. Naturally she should – well, what should she do? She knew herself. She was no proud, heroic character who could be a 'self-supporting, single mother' and disregard the prejudices of others. Maybe single and self-supporting, but not mother. Not this way, in any case. A ball and chain to a man – an obligation! She had always imagined that someday they would part with neither tears nor regrets, something like: Thank you for the time we have spent together. But later, much later, as much later as possible. Evenings without him? The city lights and fun without him?

She stood up in her stained cotton coat, nauseous and uneasy and – and something else she didn't have a name for, which was hers alone. But didn't she leave him alone with his tooth abscess? Hot compresses, and, for that matter, also pregnancy, belong to marriage, and if she wasn't going to have its pleasantries, then she didn't want to be bothered with its difficulties. Even though Bent had never talked about it, she could tell he was fond of his child, that he was a fine father and husband. It was simply a side of him which had nothing to do with her (but which she was definitely helping to maintain). With a tiny dash of bitterness, she thought about how nice it must be to return to a well-ordered home after the embraces of a lover.

'Next!'

Spindly and erect, with dark circles under her eyes, she walked reluctantly into the dimly lit room. Her heart, which should have been rational and hard, was hammering with anxiety and defiance.

He barely looked at her. He was sitting at a desk, half in shadow, without a lab coat, as she had imagined. He lazily gestured with his hand toward an empty chair. Her lips were dry, and for a few minutes neither of them said anything. The man stared out the window while he drummed on the desktop with a pencil. His dark eyebrows met in the middle, but Alice only saw his hands, which were large and hairy, and for that moment she was horrified at the thought that he was going to touch her.

When he was finished with his calculations, he suddenly

tossed down the pencil and turned to face her. He bit vigorously into his bottom lip and finally asked:

'So what is the matter?'

She wet her lips with her tongue and cleared her throat.

'I – am going to have a baby,' she said quietly, adding, before thinking about it: 'You know that very well.'

'How should I know that?' he asked with voice like a scratchy record.

A helpless feeling came over Alice. She had been told that she should 'go about it carefully', and before she had come, it had all seemed so clear to her, so right and natural; but even the man's appearance and manner gave her a sense of shame, of something unclean and terrible. She didn't understand anything, herself least of all, when she answered:

'Isn't that what you do for a living?'

She had snubbed the lifeline the man had extended. She had done something irrevocable, something whose consequences she couldn't foresee. Her reason had abandoned her.

The man's expression was vacant and uncomprehending. Without looking at her, he took out a smudged handkerchief and started cleaning his eyeglasses very energetically.

'I don't understand at all what you mean,' he said flatly.

Then the words came out by themselves, as if they had always been somewhere in the world, waiting for her, as if the entire situation had been constructed and laid out in advance – perhaps as long as she had been alive – and little could be changed about it, as much as wishful thinking could change the weather tomorrow.

She straightened herself in the chair and smoothed out her dress, over her flat belly, which would soon start swelling unmercifully.

'I mean,' she said calmly, 'this is the first time, you understand, and – and – don't I have to be examined or something?'

He rose with a gracefulness that one would never have thought possible of such a body, and it seemed to Alice that a kind of comic annoyance or impatience was evident in his movements, as he walked past her in the tiny room, where there stood a gurney.

'If you undress, I will examine you. Go right ahead.'

Her knees were shaking a little as she followed him, very erect and pale. She thought to herself, *I will often need to remember the triumph of this moment.*

Five minutes later they were sitting across from one another again. He looked at her askance over his glasses. A crooked smile quivered at the edge of his mouth. She put all the contempt she possibly could into her expression, but she couldn't make his smile go away.

Then he said slowly, with a slight, ironic bow in her direction:

'You are about three months along – congratulations, Madam.'

Then they both got up, and he reached out his hand. Childishly, she pretended not see it as she opened her purse and took out her wallet. 'How much do I owe you?'

'Twenty kroner, please.'

He held the door open for her as she left the consultation room.

'Next!' he shouted.

Not until she was down on the street, where people brushed into her impatiently on their way home for dinner, did she feel like herself again, her horrified soul reeling for support like a drunkard. Something Bent had once said occurred to her: It's not our words that reveal our character, it's the deeds we undertake, regardless of their logic. What did his child look like? The thought had never occurred to her before. A pain she had never felt before was burrowing and burning inside her. The deeds we undertake –

Slowly, with her hands in her pockets and her shiny hair blowing in the wind, she walked home to her lonely rented room.

Evening

Hanne was only seven, but she already possessed a great deal of formless anxiety. She always wanted to be somewhere other than where she was at that moment. When she sat in the nursery with her little brother, who was completely absorbed with playing, she would listen for her father's and mother's steps downstairs and do what she could to follow their strange conversation. They spoke differently with each other when they were alone than when she was listening. Her mother's voice went delicate and quiet, which made her own belly feel both nice and bad – mostly bad – and her father laughed at what her mother said almost all the time. If Hanne came jumping or sneaking down the stairs, they went completely quiet. Then her mother might say, 'How about going out to play, honey?' And if Hanne walked over to her, she didn't put her on her lap or tell her stories, but went kind of stiff, so Hanne herself became nearly immobile, feeling her father's expression wrap a dark cloak of anxiety around both of them. Then her mother said, without looking at her, 'How about going back up and playing with your little brother? Your daddy's tired.' But that wasn't true at all, because he could just go to bed and sleep, like other people did when they were tired, and he wasn't even the one who said it. He never said much to Hanne, and when he did, he just asked what two times twenty was, or if she had learned to read yet, but he didn't always listen to how she answered.

Still, he was a nice daddy, because he had never hit her or yelled at her at all, and she knew he went to work every day to earn money for clothes and food for all of them, and it would be the most horrible thing if he left them. Her mother had explained this to her one day when Hanne suddenly said, 'Oh, Daddy is so stupid,' when she saw him turn in through the garden gate on his bicycle, just as they were having such a cozy time, she and her Mommy.

There was so much to be afraid of and to be careful about. First and foremost, she had to watch her little brother, who could get strangled in his baby carriage harness or who could grab a few matches and set himself or the whole house on fire. Hanne could never relax except when she was sleeping at night, when she was relieved of her anxiousness. Not because she would be so heartbroken if her little brother died, but her mother would be so terribly sad and she would cry for days and days, just like back when Hanne's real father left them, and everything was so cheerless until they got a new one.

When they had guests, her mother laughed while she told the story of Hanne running up to window cleaners and different men she saw to ask them if they would marry her mother. Hanne didn't think it was funny, because without a daddy in the house, they would die of hunger. And she had no interest in dying and going down in the ground with no blanket over her at night. Evidently you turned into an angel and could fly up to God, but what if he came too late with your wings because there were too many others who died just at that moment, and he had to take care of all of them himself, just like her mother, since now they didn't have enough money for a nanny?

Her little brother was sleeping, and Hanne lay scratching the paint off her bed's blue rails. She never fell asleep before she heard her mother and father go to bed, and sometimes not until they had stopped talking in their bedroom and she was sure they were sleeping, so nothing could change during the course of the night.

They were still talking, down in the living room. Their quiet alone-voices, with her father's laughter and long pauses in between, made her head hurt, like when her little brother dumped all his blocks down on the floor at once. Maybe they were kissing one another, because that was part of being married, but not when the children are looking, because it's not good for them. 'Wait until we're alone,' her mother said once. 'It would be a sin for the child to see us.' Why would it be a sin? Sin had something to do with God and bedtime prayers.

Hanne lay down on her back and folded her hands on top of the comforter. Then God was in the room, but you couldn't see him, even if you turned on the light. Hanne imagined that he looked like her real father, who was the biggest and strongest man in the whole world. She closed her eyes and whispered the best of all bedtime prayers:

> Now I lay down in my bed
> close my eyes and bow my head
> Dear Lord, please look down with grace
> upon our shabby rented place.

Then she sighed, sleepy and serene, until her thoughts came streaming back like hungry birds to a spring garden bed.

If only they would come upstairs soon. Hanne's eyes were starting to smart. The day after tomorrow was Sunday, and she was going to visit her real father and his new wife, who was much prettier than her mother, but still repulsive. Goodness knows her father didn't really love her, because they didn't have any children, and people only had children if they loved each other very much, like her mother loved her new father, back when she had her little brother. But luckily that passed, because after that there were no more babies who could be strangled by their harnesses or who could set the house on fire. Loving someone couldn't be helped. It came and went like whooping cough. But it was no use if only one person was the loving one, and that was a good thing, because Hanne loved her math teacher and her real father and her mother of course, and of the three she was only certain that her father loved her back. And she couldn't marry her father since he was old, like she would be when she grew up and got breasts and things like that, and you couldn't get married before then. If only she had been just as big as her father's new wife, whom she was supposed to call Grete-mom, when she stayed with them. But her father just called her Grete. Boy, was she dumb. And she had so many fancy dresses, a lot more than her mother. 'Don't worry about that,' her mother said. 'Only dumb people concern themselves with dressing up all the time.' But that her father, who was so smart, liked to kiss and be nice to such a dummy! Even though she had those long curls and eyes that always looked damp, as if she had just been crying. And she always laughed at everything, even when Hanne misbehaved. Last time she was there, Grete had put on a long silk gown with nothing on top, and spun around in front of Hanne and said, 'Don't you think I look pretty?' And Hanne had borrowed a joke from her limited, newly acquired vocabulary from school: 'Yes! From behind and in the dark!' But then they had both laughed so much that Hanne ended up crying and had to be comforted on her father's lap like a little baby, and she drew out her crying until Grete-mom stopped laughing. Served her right!

Hanne sniffled and pulled her handkerchief out from under her pillow. She blew her nose and rubbed it afterward, which she wasn't supposed to do, because then her nostrils would get big and open and the rain would go right in them. 'I don't care,' she said aloud, like when she hurt herself and didn't cry. She meant it about a lot of things. There were lots of things you could say 'I don't care' about. About Grete-mom, about if little brother got strangled, about her new father who mustn't leave them, about if he did leave, about if they got a new one –

Suddenly she sat up in bed with her heart pounding. There was a new voice in the living room. A loud, happy, loving and familiar voice, which sounded just the same whether you were there or not. But it couldn't be. Why would he come here? She listened. It was really *him*. He had come to chase out the new father and marry her mother again. Grete-mom must have died. Then her mother would get all her pretty dresses. She jumped out of bed and pulled up on her nightgown and raced down the stairs. 'Daddy!' she shouted, seeing nothing but him as, blinded by the light, she ran right into his tall body and let herself be enveloped in his familiar smell and touch in a blessed, all-shielding embrace. Then she blinked her eyes and looked at her father and mother who slowly solidified into two stiff, distant figures outside her world.

'Your daddy wants you to go with him now,' said her mother with a slight unfamiliar quaver in her voice. 'Go upstairs and get dressed, Hanne, but be careful not to wake up your little brother.'

There were three coffee cups on the table, and the living room seemed smaller than usual.

Her father straightened up, still with one hand on the girl's neck. She bored a finger into one of his buttonholes and spun it around. Her whole body felt warm, as if she had just been in a bath.

'Aren't you going to stay here, Daddy?' she whispered anxiously, staring up into his big bright eyes.

Then her new father stood up and violently pushed in his chair.

'Couldn't this have waited until tomorrow?' he said in a thin, sharp voice. 'Who tears a child out of bed at this time of night?'

Her father didn't answer, but bent down again and pulled her close. 'Wouldn't you like to go on a trip with Grete-mom and me?' he asked. 'She's out in the car.'

Then Hanne went as stiff as her mother. 'Isn't she dead?' she asked, her mouth going dry.

'But Hanne, dear,' said her mother. 'Don't talk like that. You don't have to go if you don't want to.' And her father released her suddenly, as if he had burned himself. For a moment he stood there alone, not knowing what to do with his hands or his eyes. Then her new father took her hand and started leading her up the stairs, while the silence behind them hurt just as much as his hard, unfamiliar grasp. She didn't want to cry before she was in bed. No, she wasn't going to cry; she wasn't even going to bed. She was going on a trip and she was going to sit on her father's lap the whole way.

'Let me go!' she yelled, twisting her hand out of the man's grip and running back into the sharp light, where her mother sat, looking pitiful, and where there was a father too many. Something unmerciful, a totally new anxiety, kept her from seeking the most comforting shelter she knew. She stood hanging her head in front of her father, who had put on his hat, as if his work here was finished. She felt cold and shrugged her spindly shoulders and stepped hard on her own toes, as she gazed helplessly and imploringly at her mother, who was looking up at the man on the stairway with an anxious, pleading expression, as if it were she who had said something wrong.

He walked down the stairs with hard, deliberate steps. 'Let's get this over with right now,' he said tersely. 'Are you coming or not, Hanne?'

She looked down at her father's feet. Her forehead was burning with confusion, shame, and defiance. She took the difficult steps toward him, but he didn't touch her. His clothes smelled of distant, lost things. The whole way she could sit and sleep with her nose buried in his smell with her back to Grete-mom.

'I – want to come,' she begged, humbled with defeat.

When the girl went upstairs to get dressed, three people watched her lonely little figure. None of them could help her, and they didn't dare look at one another.

Depression

Lulu stacked the dirty dishes on top of one another in the nearly scalding water, so parsley sprigs, wilted lettuce leaves, and radish tops released and floated on top in a sad, greasy stew, which she appraised, disgusted for a moment, before she could bring herself to plunge her hands down into it and bring the porcelain back out. First the plates, then the forks, knives, and glasses. She used a lot of water. Behind her, the dented kettle was boiling dry, because she kept forgetting to fill it.

She heard noise and laughter from the living room. It was a festive, successful evening, and she knew it made a little dip in the mood when she, the hostess, in the middle of all the merriment, broke away to do the dishes. But she couldn't face waking up in the morning to a messy kitchen. Kai would just have to figure it out. She could hear his voice among the others; he spoke quickly, nervously, excitedly. He drank and smoked like crazy, and forgot to be accommodating to the guests when she wasn't around.

It would be so wonderful if his depression were over and done with. It had lasted from the moment they realized she was definitely pregnant for the second time in their marriage.

The first depression lasted until she was five months along. And now little Bent was only one and a half. Of course it was unfortunate, but to her mind it wasn't the end of the world. And certainly not for him. In the end, she was the one who had to do the heavy lifting. But she was, as Kai put it, so healthy and well-adjusted. The nausea, the exhaustion, and everything that came with it, she knew would come to an end shortly. The economic stress would have to be borne by Kai (or more correctly, his parents), and unlike her complaints, that would only increase after the baby was born.

His studies would be finished in a year. But he had done no work for the last three months; he just lay all day long on the divan without sleeping or doing anything. If she tiptoed through the living room, he gave her a pained, unhappy look, which made her feel guilty, because she never knew if she should lie down beside him and caress his forehead, or if that would just bother him.

He went to psychoanalysis, but she didn't think it was helping. On the contrary, it cost a fortune, and this stranger (his analyst), whom she had never seen, instilled in her a distrust and something resembling jealousy. He had suggested admittance to an institution, but Kai didn't want that, because of his parents, who lived at their parsonage in Jylland and supported them, and who mustn't at any cost be upset by bad news from Copenhagen. He was their only child, and they expected a result from investing in their son in the form of a newly hatched doctor.

Every time he had gone to psychoanalysis, Kai showed animosity toward her and Bent afterward, and he was more irritable than usual. If she didn't know better, she would think he had returned from being with another woman. Sometimes she wished it were something like that. At least that was something you could wrap your head around, a battle you could win or lose. The way it was now, it was like some strong, invisible enemy was sapping her energy, but she wasn't supposed to feel that way. Sometimes Kai tried to discuss it with her. 'It's important that one person in the world totally understands why I react the way I do,' he explained.

During his first depression, Kai had begun studying 'mental mechanisms' and things like that; and when he started to brighten up again, he would only spend time with people who were involved in similar pursuits. They were studying for a test (she didn't know what the subject was) or had already taken it. They often (no, almost exclusively) spoke with tortured faces about the doctors' distrust of them, and they challenged Kai to 'do something for their cause' in his medical capacity. She had the vague feeling that they were in the process of seducing him into something mystical of which she could never be a part, since she, according to their 'teaching', could never understand or help him, because she was too close. But when his mood changed, and suddenly he wanted to have people around him, he gushed with brightness and attentiveness. 'You have been so amazing,' he said then. 'How would I have ever gotten through this without you?'

Lulu sat down for a minute on the kitchen counter and wearily brushed her hair back from her forehead with her hand. Kai's voice reached her from the living room: 'The essential difference between a depression and a neurosis . . .'

She jumped down and started putting things away, rattling them unnecessarily loudly. They always talked like that. Psychoanalysis, repression, hypnosis, depression, neurosis, mania! Sometimes she actually felt guilty over her own boring psyche, and found herself rather lacking, that in the middle of a crazy and besieged world she could keep her grip on the insignificant, necessary things which formed the foundation of their existence. But she was incurably normal, even though Kai asserted at times that she was full of inhibitions and complexes which she wouldn't acknowledge. 'The way the world looks today,' he said, 'it's more a wonder that a person can keep their ego together, than that they give up.' He looked at her with a cool, questioning face, as if she were a kitten playing in the middle of a pile of smoldering ruins. She wondered how he would take it if one day she 'gave up'!

Lulu removed her apron and walked to the bathroom to straighten her appearance a bit before returning to their guests. God knows if they would be gone by midnight. Kai slept so poorly, despite the sleeping pills and sedatives; but for the time being it didn't matter that he wasn't sleeping. He woke her early in the morning and was innocent, happy, and full of pep, kissing her lovingly and playing with Bent and laying out the wildest plans for the future. She had become used to hearing about them, and she listened in the same way that she listened to the child's excited, awkward babbling. They would have their own house, or a farm with blue shutters and a thatched roof, a puppy at least – people could learn a lot from animals: give them neuroses, create conditioned reflexes, etc. Anyway it was wrong the way they walled themselves in and never saw other people. It wasn't healthy for her either –

He was like that this morning, and he had called far and wide to invite people over. All day he had helped her prepare for the party. Everything was bought on credit; everything always got paid for at the last possible moment. She had to take detours so she wouldn't pass the stores where they were in debt. Owing money didn't bother Kai, who was otherwise so picky about things. But it bothered her enormously.

Inviting people over and filling them with food and wine that hadn't been paid for took away half the enjoyment for her. But she had been happy most of the day, because Kai was. He opened cans, brought the wine to room temperature, and gave her advice with regards to spices and vegetables that would liven up the table.

In the midst of all their preparations, Kai sat down with Bent on his lap, testing the boy in various ways to display his intelligence. Bent was in good form today, and the child was jubilant when he guessed right. 'Daddy happy!' he shouted, and Kai was moved and thoughtful a moment, as he set the child down in the playpen. 'It's a shame it affects other people when you feel a certain way,' he said. In her hands, tenderly, she had taken his fine, narrow face, which already bore the indelible mark of his secret inner pain, from which she couldn't relieve him. 'A day like today offsets this whole, long, difficult period for all of us,' she said softly.

But it was so hard to stay on his wavelength for an extended period. He pulled a book down from the shelf and read aloud to her – one of his study books, replete with red underlining – while she stood over a pan of scrambled eggs. She could detect in his voice when she should smile or nod understandingly. She felt like an idiot. The words didn't really reach her; she just listened for the excitement and intensity in his voice, and she thought about a thousand other things at the same time: How was she going to seat nine people at the dining table? They were short two glasses, and one was chipped, but she could use that one. With some goodwill, three people could sit on the divan.

Kai approached the boy again – something about drawings from the book he wanted to try. An ugly face and a nice face. 'Which one of these two faces that you see here is ugly, and which one is nice?' She awaited the result anxiously. Kai's spindly, stooping figure appeared in the kitchen doorway; his forehead was wrinkled. 'I don't understand,' he said. 'A two-year-old child should be able to handle that, and Bent is so gifted! Maybe there is some defect in that test.'

But soon he forgot all about it and bounded down the steps to get a head of celery. You couldn't offer people cheese without celery stalks!

Even before the guests arrived, she was unable to hide her exhaustion. Her hair was limp from the steam in the kitchen; her only decent dress was tight around the middle. The energetic, perfectly made-up young women (women in that circle never studied so hard that it detracted from their looks) she let in made her feel ugly and awkward. When they had all settled in, they sat for an hour or so, smoking and chatting, and each time Lulu left the room, Kai shouted, 'Where are you going now? Relax. Stay here with us.' 'He's like a chicken without a head when you aren't in the room,' teased one of the women, while she looked at Kai with steady, beaming eyes. He was like another person. A white shirt ironed at the last second, and a rare humorous glint in his eye that she could only recall from when they were engaged. Something he never lavished on her alone. Why not? He loved her; he was dependent on her, but he also loved the endearment of others. He was like a vain child – a difficult child.

Stepping back into the living room, she blinked slightly at the light, and her gaze sought out Kai's. Now he was elated, totally happy, the center of the group's attention. He was talking non-stop, his thin fingers outlining curves in the air when he wanted to explain something. All the bottles and glasses were empty. The tablecloth was stained with red wine and gravy, the air was thick and close from the smoke. She sat down, without anyone seeming to notice. In any case, they didn't take their eyes off Kai – neither the men nor the women. She felt a sudden urge to close her eyes and go to sleep. A dark-haired woman, whom she recognized from the summer, when they had held study circles in psychology once a week, smiled at her and made room next to her on the divan. 'You look tired, Lulu,' she said sympathetically. Appalled, Lulu straightened up on her seat and smiled vacantly. 'I'm not tired at all,' she said quickly, and in the same breath, 'Isn't it great that Kai is doing so well?'

They both looked at him. Then the young woman said warmly, 'He's smarter than any of us. It's a shame if he doesn't get the most out of his ability.'

Lulu didn't answer. Was it her fault if he didn't get the most out of his ability? Had her loving and all too fertile body pulled him down into the banal and boring? The psycho-analyst was supposed to free him from guilt, but who was going to free her? She was still looking at her husband. His thin, well-proportioned frame, his burning eyes, the words streaming from his beautifully arched lips. Yes, he was happy now, she thought; these people idolize him; he doesn't need me. And after they've left, it occurred to her, he will keep me awake the rest of the night talking about the party, and I will have to say that his friends are absolutely the most fabulous people – everything he loves I have to admire too, while also knowing that I don't measure up to them – but I am all alone with the baby I'm carrying. If he mentions it at all, it's as an increased expense – a bill from the butcher, or an oppressive creditor.

Everyone was talking all around her, over her head, and the bitterness was overflowing without her being able to stop it, filling her mind and senses with poisonous steam. She didn't understand why, and she had never felt like this before. She had always been so gracious in excusing him, and for months she had stood guard between him and the outside world. Kept her family and girlfriends at bay with all kinds of pretenses, sent friends away when they appeared at the door, endlessly empathetic: 'Is he depressed again? Dear God, what that man is up against!' She had even taken it out on Bent, when he'd been rambunctious: 'Daddy needs peace and quiet!'

This wasn't what she had imagined when they got married. But what that was, she wasn't really sure. A girlfriend had brought them together: 'A devastatingly handsome and smart guy is coming tonight; you absolutely have to meet him!'

The 'devastatingly handsome guy' was back now. He was talking with a pale young man whom Lulu didn't care for, because he always asked with such earnestness if she 'was doing well', and after an affirmative answer, would turn away with a doubtful, knowing expression, as if no one, according to his definition, could go around 'doing well'; and if it really were the case, he wasn't the least bit interested. For his part, he had the look of someone who suffered from constant indigestion; Kai was speaking to this person fervently, bent toward and directly facing him, in the way that a child is completely absorbed with something nearby. 'Psychiatrists won't acknowledge the analytical method,' he said, 'but they will have to eventually, you can bet on that. Not one of them has the least grasp of what they're dealing with.'

Lulu's bitterness congealed into a small, hard knot, there, where her heart usually sat. She stood up all of a sudden, pale, and without looking at any of the others. 'Do you mind if I head to bed? I'm exhausted,' she said, loudly and clearly, and there was a brief silence in the room. Kai finally stared at her with an angry, cold, irritated, and somewhat confused expression in his eyes.

'You're tired?' he asked, as if she had said something unseemly, unheard of, almost indecent. Then he wrinkled his forehead and brushed his hand through his hair, bewildered, as if he were seeking aid against an injustice that had been leveled at him. The men looked at the women; the women at the men. A kind of collusion sprang up among them, brushing Lulu aside, but she held herself erect and expressionless as they stood up and said goodbye.

When the door was shut behind the last one, he turned toward her angrily. 'What the devil are you doing?' he shouted. 'Don't you have the most basic decency?' He looked like he wanted to hit her. Then he saw her face was wet with tears, slowly slipping out between her eyelashes, and he observed her a moment, full of wonder. He had never seen her cry before. Sheepishly, he led her to the divan, where she pulled close to him, shaking with sobs and exhaustion like a small animal seeking protection. He got a blanket and laid it over her. He stood up, observing her, fragile and bent. The gleam in his eye was gone, the party was over. Outside, the birds were starting to sing. He got down on one knee and caressed her hair. She took his hand and put it to her cheek, and looked up at him helplessly and inquisitively, but he gently pulled his hand back.

'We are quite a pair,' he said quietly, more to himself than to her.

BOOK TWO

The Trouble with Happiness

The Knife

He lay there intensely observing his sleeping wife, as if she represented a mathematical problem which needed solving before he could move on to other things. He always felt a certain tenderness toward her just before he woke her in the morning. But this passed quickly, and she rarely noticed it. He heard their son padding around in the nursery, coughing quietly and talking to himself. Their son knew it was strictly forbidden to wake his parents.

He turned toward the wall and shouted, 'Okay, Esther, it's eight o'clock!'

This was his usual morning greeting. One of the duties he adopted, for some obscure reason, was to show his family a cool and slightly accusatory tone, which was supposed to express his general attitude toward life, and reinforce his own estimation of himself as a rational person who disdained sentimentality. He didn't have his wife's picture on his desk at his office, and, unlike his colleagues, he didn't walk around with little photographs of his offspring to flaunt at any time. Still, they were both almost constantly in his thoughts, though the actual nature of the relationship was difficult for him to determine, just as he found it hard to differentiate one from the other. They existed like shadows inside him, thought-fetuses he couldn't get rid of, products of a weakness in him which he tried with all his might to overcome. They were in the way of his plans, and they made him distracted and irritable, precisely at times when he needed to harness his energy. He often thought: My life would have evolved quite differently if they weren't around. He had still been studying when he met Esther. He wasn't really sure if he would have married her if it hadn't suddenly become necessary. This was a question he asked himself many times a day, without ever finding an answer, or delving into what value such an answer would have for him, considering how things stood. But he didn't like the idea that his life could be determined by chance. Things and people were something you reached out for, when they could be useful to a certain end. Either you used them for something, or else you risked being used by them.

He sat up in bed looking silently at his wife, who was sitting in her slip, combing her hair in front of her dressing table, unconcerned about her half-nakedness, as if they had been married for twenty-five years. She smiled at him in the mirror, hesitantly, guiltily, a bearing that was a natural reaction to his, but didn't annoy him any less.

'Why in the world don't you get dressed before doing your hair?' he asked crossly.

Without responding, she stood up and went into the nursery. In a tone as if he were still a baby, she said, 'Good morning, honey.'

She was spoiling that boy. She was sucking all the independence right out of his body with her motherly fuss, but he would show them both – though he wasn't really sure yet what he would 'show' them. He looked at his watch, hopped out of bed, and sneezed five or six times before putting on his clothes. He always had morning congestion. It wasn't a cold; it was due to nerves, the doctor had said. Before he was married he didn't have any ailments.

He walked out to the bathroom; he could hear her moving around in the kitchen. She was filling the kettle. Carefully he let the razor blade glide over his protruding Adam's apple. The boy was noticeably quiet. Had he gone back to bed? Usually he was at his mother's heels in the morning, babbling on and on about all kinds of things. It was kind of interesting to listen to what children say when they don't know anyone's listening. He realized with surprise that he almost missed that babbling. Half our lives is habit, he thought.

She was spooning out oatmeal for their son when he entered the dining room. She glanced at him. 'I'll get the coffee,' she said.

He gave a quick nod and sat down across from his son and took a look at him. The child avoided his gaze and rocked nervously in his chair.

He must have done something, thought the father.

A certain suspicion occurred to him. He grimaced as if he had just tasted something bitter.

'Can you show Daddy your knife?' he said gently.

The boy had been given the knife for Christmas. Since then, the father had asked about it every now and then. The boy didn't keep track of his things well enough, and when one of his toys got lost, his mother replaced it with the same thing, as well as she could, to avoid conflict. A short-sighted, egotistical maneuver, which furthermore was somewhat pointless, because the switch was usually discovered. Apart from a few instances which involved a cowboy pistol, a headband with an Indian feather, and a plastic puzzle, he was always able to expose her tricks. It really didn't take much brainpower to tell the difference between new and used things. The other three times he hadn't mentioned anything. He had a strong sense of justice, and would rather risk believing a lie than blaming people for things they hadn't done.

But the knife was another matter entirely. He had received it from his own father when he was six years old; and when he handed it over to his son on Christmas Eve, he had explicitly impressed on the boy that ownership of the knife came with certain responsibilities. Contrary to the boy's other possessions, this one was utterly irreplaceable. Whenever he asked the boy to get it, all three of them gazed at the intricately engraved blade and the worn sheath with devotion resulting from the awareness that, for the husband, the sight of the knife brought back many treasured memories. He explained how he had always worn it in his Boy Scout belt, and it made him feel superior to the other boys who didn't have a knife like that. Both the boy and his mother knew it was the gift – and back then children weren't so pampered, and he didn't get many gifts – he valued most in his whole life. Now he had passed it on to his son, who had just turned five, and in order to do that, he had taken good care of it his entire life. At least that's how it seemed to him now.

The boy looked at him, horrified, and his face reddened. His big eyes filled with anxious tears.

'It – it's lost,' he whispered.

He clutched the spoon and his little knuckles turned white.

The mother poured coffee in her husband's cup. Her hand shook.

'I'm sure we'll find it,' she said quickly.

He took some sugar and cream and stirred his coffee, while

she stood beside him twisting her apron nervously between her fingers. He looked up at her with pursed lips.

'So you knew about this,' he said coldly. 'How long did you think it would take for me to find out?'

His heart was beating loud and hard with anger. Well, isn't this great, he thought.

He sat down next to the boy, who was still sitting with his hand clenched around the spoon, without eating.

'It got lost yesterday,' she said, looking down at the table-cloth. 'I figured we would find it again, since it's happened before. Go ahead and eat your oatmeal, honey.'

She patted the boy on the head.

He went out to the entry and got his coat.

'I suggest you find it by tonight,' he said.

He left without saying goodbye.

All day long he thought about the lost knife. Back when he was a little boy, he used to walk the overgrown path in the woods behind his parents' house. His knife gleamed in the air before him, sunshine glancing off the blade. He cut willow sticks with it. Drunk with power, he decided which branches he would spare, and which would fall before his knife. Some of those he cut were weak and inadequate, and he couldn't use them. Sometimes he decided that a strong, vigorous branch would be allowed to survive. The willow branches were enemies in a defeated army. Decisively and capriciously he cut them down. Proudly, he showed his treasure to another little boy and let him feel its weight in his hand. The boy gave it back to him as if it were nothing special. Big clouds passed overhead. Others didn't understand that he was meant for something glorious and triumphant. When he felt the knife against his hip, he was strong and alone in the wilderness. It had been bought in Finland. His father had brought it home from a business trip. There wasn't another knife like it in all of Denmark. He played 'Country' with some friends, stabbing the knife angrily into the ground like it was the heart of his worst enemy. The blade stayed vertical, vibrating a bit with a barely audible tone. He drew a circle around himself on the ground. 'I'll kill anyone who steps over this line,' he shouted. No one tried to step over the line. They chatted peacefully on the outside and let him stand inside the circle, swinging his knife. He didn't care about the games they played, and they didn't understand his. Even before he started school he had developed a taste for being alone. He felt it was a sign that he was different than the others, selected by fate as a person who would do great things. He talked out loud to himself on the way to school when no one was around. He was an army general conferring with enemy heads of state. He formulated his words craftily and deviously, borrowing them from Carit Etlar's and Ingemann's novels. He was good at world history. For a long time Napoleon was his hero. He thought Napoleon must have been like his father, a quiet, strict man, with an unpredictable and puzzling nature. His mother talked a lot, often confusingly. Suddenly she would go quiet and look at his father. They never fought. Still there was something secretive between them. He had felt, in some obscure way, that they were enemies, and he sided with his father. He sat between them in the evening, looking at his knife. It wasn't a toy, but a weapon made to be used at the proper time. Finnish sailors always carried knives just like it.

He carried out his work as usual, and gave orders to the women in the office. A strange, dark excitement came over him. Now was the time to act, conclusively, radically. He wasn't going to spoil his son. Suddenly he saw the little scared face in his mind's eye, and he felt something like compassion, which he flatly rejected. The knife sliced an invisible path through his thoughts and cut away everything that was superfluous and dangerously weak. He was going to be the pillar in the boy's upbringing – the seriousness, the sense of responsibility. But the boy always ran and hid behind his mother. If this kept up, he would have a rough life. He had the same weakness in his face that she did.

He pursed his lips and wrinkled his brow. I did warn them, he thought. I have tolerated plenty. As the day passed, it felt like something was slowly coming loose inside him, something which for a long time had been accumulating and weighing unbearably on his mind. They had created a world without him, even though it was only because of him that they existed at all. They were afraid of him and shrank from him. Tonight he would show who was in charge – the only one in the world who could properly protect his son. Losing the knife was the last straw. He had the vague notion that he had already seen this coming when he gave it to the boy. That boy lost everything. He didn't value things that cost money. And who supplied the money? In his mind he had a foggy vision of himself as an aging man with a spineless failure of a son, whose excesses and debts he would have to pay. And his wife was always swarming around the boy, defending him, trying to hide his mistakes, acting guilty and distant, adrift in motherhood, lost, unreachable by anyone but her son. This can't continue. He was a strong, rational person who was not going to be controlled by chance. He was the one who would be in control. He would utilize every opportunity that appeared, make connections, and without scruples leap past those with seniority. But people

'Daddy,' he yelled, panting, 'we found the knife. I left it at Preben's house!'

Caught off guard, he stared down at his son. His shoulders sank almost imperceptibly. Something inside him collapsed like a house of cards. He mechanically took the boy's hand.

'Well, that was good,' he said flatly. His heart was pounding erratically, like after a long run. His legs felt heavy. His clear, incisive thoughts condensed suddenly into a dense, impenetrable thicket. Something toppled inside him with dizzying velocity, a hope, perhaps. Nothing was changed; maybe change wasn't possible. Upstairs his wife was waiting. She would show him the knife with relief. As always, she and the boy would stand in the kitchen talking quietly, while he sat there waiting for the food, grumbling, lonely, irritated.

The boy peered up at him, concerned. He had to skip along to keep up with his father's long strides.

'Why don't you look happy, Daddy?' he asked anxiously.

He didn't get an answer.

The Method

Being married to an entire person was too much. It was too much to grasp. It was intimidating, overwhelming. She didn't know how he could stand it, or when his method started. She figured everyone had their own method, inasmuch as it was endured, by and large. People found their method just when they were about to be crushed, before it was too late. Adapting a little at a time was hers; then things would be fine for a long while, until the method's unresolved limit was reached. It was that dangerous area right around his nose, and, well, the nose itself, which she couldn't handle. When the days of the nose arrived, she tried avoiding them, first by distracting herself, then with anxious, fake joviality: No, no, my friend, we'll skip over you just this once. Goodness knows, who hasn't been forced to stand in a corner or been a bench warmer one happy evening? It's part of life, it's the way the world is. She would try starting from scratch with the hands. But that never worked. The hands were deeply insulted and distant, in solidarity with the nose. Amazing how a body teams up so obstinately! Demands fairness. She let go of his hand and seized on his eyes, which stared cruelly at her, glassy and omniscient. It wouldn't be their turn for a week. Her final option was to open all her pores and breathe in the whole person, a risky, suffocating moment, where a burnt smell of unfamiliar childhood seared her and curled her into an amoeba-like ball of simple self-maintenance. When, with difficulty, she crawled around the room, and little by little retrieved all the parts of her personality and patched them back together (though usually a few small fasteners were missing, which she later would find hidden away in cracks in the paneling or under the shelf liner in the pantry, and think indifferently that it was all part of his method, which wasn't any of her business), his nose was noticeably softened and let itself be passed up without any particular resistance. This process was exhausting and caused her violent mood swings, which often drove her to seek reconciliation with the nose. She suggested they adopt a peaceful and vegetative truce, a friendly sibling relationship, a vigilant attentiveness toward handkerchiefs, with particular regard for the nose's special interests, which of course were often ignored by the owner; but it was all in vain. The nose would settle for nothing less than love. It made such a nuisance of itself that, at a certain point, she changed the sequence and put it after the eye-days, which were the best of the month. She really loved the eyes and told them so without letting herself be disturbed by the voice, which ran in its own channel, completely satisfied with the formation of the couple upon the thin ice of the surface; satisfied with those days which belonged to it alone, with periodic certainty. She loved the eyes and gave herself to them and let their soft gleam penetrate deep inside her, so that for seconds at a time she forgot the threatening cliff on the lower level. To bolster her further, she added a vacation day between the eyes and the nose. After some practice, the trick worked. The man didn't realize that he wasn't there. He must never discover this, because it would have made his method impossible, regardless what it consisted of. They always respected one another's methods without knowing the slightest bit about them, which is very common between people. But when the vacation day was over, that stupid lump of flesh was there again with its unavoidable demand. She should love it, take it in as her own. It stuck out of the bag when she was shopping. It clogged the keyhole, so it was as if the key had been made to fit a much smaller opening. In its cruel jadedness, the nose caused her countless small exasperations and pursued her nightly in her dreams in the most terrifying disguises. Only a few times over the course of the years had she been able to collect herself and avoid it. She might have been able to bear the enmity of the hands, the forehead, the ankles, and the shoulders, but not the eyes. For their sake she now always chose the dismembering escape route of the shatter-mechanism, and she got used to overlooking the nose's vibrating insult, to the extent the eyes failed to see it. But she was never blind to the danger of her method. Another woman, she thought, would have probably found a better solution. A blotting-paper woman would have devoured him completely with no trouble, without even spitting out the hair and bones, and then she would have lain herself in a secret drawer, where everything was ready and well-kept, humidity retained by preserving fluid. But for her, so slippery and water-repellent, this method was the only one. Danger lay in the nose's dissatisfaction, and in time she saw the situation approaching catastrophe. Her fate became unbearable; something had to give. It started insidiously. One morning when she was crawling around, blubbering and dispossessed, fumbling for her centrifugally split ego, she realized there were three nails missing as well as two gears,

meaningless in themselves and which she rarely used. Ridden
with anxiety she looked in the usual hiding places, and then
all over the house, in the cellar, in the attic, and finally under
the bushes and trees in the yard. All in vain. They were and
would remain lost, and she never found them again. Not
that anyone noticed. It wasn't the kind of loss the world paid
attention to. Yes, she discovered, her scalp tingling with fear,
what a great deal of one's self a person can lose while retain-
ing the ability to function. It wasn't until she kept falling out
of rhythm, because it was hard for her to hear the music – but
this was after a long time had passed, many, many years – that
in her desperate loneliness she sought comfort at the eyes, her
nicest friends. And when in the depth of the pupils she saw a
glint like rusty metal, it was as if a damp rag was wrapping
around her heart, and she realized that all the disappeared
things had ended up there, somewhere inside her husband,
and that he would never give them back to her, even if he
wanted to. This was simply because he had no clue about the
robbery. It was just the simple, consequential punishment
for the defective method. Then an egotistical fiery column
of horror rose up inside her, and she dropped her method
immediately and completely, from one moment to the next,
indifferent to others and determined only to preserve the few
essential parts that had not yet been stolen from her. Indifferent to 'getting through it'. The music was gone, and they
stood completely still while people jostled them. Her eyes
sought the nose, though it wasn't its time yet. She saw it had
grown bigger and was full and friendly, completely filled with
her possessions and much too busy digesting them to keep
paying her even the slightest attention. It had finally been satisfied. Its large, dilated nostrils turned away from her, and in
limp, frigid jealousy she saw that they were turned toward

Anxiety

•

The bed creaked, and she timidly looked up at the ceiling. Then she set her coffee cup down very carefully, so the spoon wouldn't clink. The bed creaked differently when he was awake. But sometimes it didn't creak at all, and that was just about the worst. This had been going on for three years now, and she never had time to remember how it had been before. He was a copy-editor and he worked at night. When he came home in the morning, she could instantly see on his face if there had been typos in the newspaper, but sometimes he didn't read it until he woke up. He got terribly angry at her when there were mistakes, and it really was a shame, she thought, since he did his work so diligently. She was careful to always think good thoughts about him. But once in a while – like now, for example – when he was awake and she was drinking coffee, she thought it would be nice if someone came by to chat. In the beginning Henny came by sometimes, because she always had. Henny was her sister, and she lived nearby. But even though they were very careful and spoke quietly, the bed creaked continually. It was the awake creaking. Henny said, 'Sound really travels in here!' So they started whispering. Then he yelled that they didn't have to whisper; he couldn't sleep anyway. And she was always glad when Henny left. It was better that way.

Actually she wanted a cat. Then she would have company at least, and cats were silent. One day, when he was in a good mood, she would ask him if she could get a cat.

She looked up at the ceiling again. It was quiet. Was he sleeping? She moved her foot and wriggled her ankle. She didn't get enough exercise. They used to go for walks together in the evenings or on Sundays. Now he stayed in bed on Sundays too. It was an old bed. It was worn more than hers, which was against the other wall. He wasn't much for marital relations.

She bent over and picked up a piece of thread from the floor. She never cleaned until he left. She bumped the table with her head, and the spoon clinked against the cup. Her face flushed and her heart started pounding. She was so clumsy. No matter how much she tried, some accident always happened. She could have just left the thread there. The bed creaked.

'Are you sitting there drinking coffee again?' he shouted.

'Oh,' she shouted back, 'did I wake you? I just warmed up what was left from this morning.'

'I heard you take the lid off the coffee tin.' His voice resounded through the ceiling. 'Drink all the coffee you want. You don't have to make up silly stories.'

She stood up with her cup in hand. She was going to carry it out to the kitchen. She listened first, in case he was going to say more. The echo of his voice was still reverberating inside her, and she couldn't move until it petered out. Then her heart calmed down again. The bed creaked loudly a few times, triumphantly.

She walked out and put down the cup first, then the spoon,

then the saucer. What he said was right. He didn't care if she drank coffee. He really was quite amiable. It wasn't his fault that he was such a light sleeper. She decided to go and visit Henny. She decided that quite often, but it rarely amounted to anything. She really enjoyed being with her sister's children, even though they were terribly noisy. She was not convinced that so much noise could be a good thing. As a kind of counterbalance she always whispered. Then Henny laughed and said she was getting to be too strange. Henny said that Arthur was making her go nutty by lying in bed and creaking all day. But where else was he supposed to go? Henny was really unreasonable.

She took a couple of hesitant steps toward the door.

'You going out gallivanting?' he shouted.

She brought her hand to her chest. Her throat was suddenly parched. She cleared her throat.

'No,' she yelled. 'Just putting on my shoes.'

'They're noisy,' he roared, and she could hear that he was about to lose his patience. She collected herself. If she didn't yell as loud as she could, he maintained, it was impossible to hear her. Otherwise his hearing was fine.

'Then I won't put them on,' she shouted desperately.

She sat back down at the table. It was quiet again up there, and ten minutes passed in charged, attentive silence. Then the quiet was interrupted by a muffled, pleasant snoring, one of the most comforting sounds in her world of sounds.

She stretched her stiff body and her joints creaked. Then she smiled and rubbed her hands together. It would be at least an hour before he woke up again. She could easily go and visit Henny and be back by then. She was alone too much. There was a time when they used to have visitors, just like other people. Her mother had sat there in that chair, her brother on the sofa beside his wife. It went well for a couple of hours. Then he started to become silent. They spoke to him and he answered with single syllable words. She didn't know how it happened, but suddenly everyone was on edge. They spoke under their breath, as if an accident had occurred, with short, anxious glances at him. Then they left, and what remained was much too much food for two people, as well as the feeling that she had committed a crime. When she returned to him after a nervous, whispered round of goodbyes in the entry, he was already asleep in his winged armchair. When he woke up, he was surprised they had left. Sometimes he too had had friends over, a couple of single young men, who sat there all evening, listening to him, while she brought in beer and carried out the empty bottles. They didn't say much themselves. In fact, they seemed slightly afraid of him. She didn't know why. But all that felt as if it had occurred on some other planet. She only thought about it when he was sleeping. While she put on her shoes and jacket, very carefully and quietly, she also thought that they should have had a child. She was too old for that now – nearly thirty-five – but back when they were still young. Though even then – on an even more distant planet – it had happened rarely. Only once in a while, in the dark and in deep silence, was he able to overcome his reluctance to that kind of thing. Afterward it was as if he was angry at her. They never talked about it.

She turned the lock before opening the door. He could always hear the little click it made. Out on the road she looked both ways before hurrying, like a thin shadow, the fifty or so steps to her sister's place.

The two children ran to her embrace.

'My, oh my,' she said, touched. 'Well, it has been a long time. And I didn't bring anything to give you.'

And they took her hands and danced around her, until she lost her breath and sat down laughing, clapping her hand over her mouth as if it were the utmost foolishness. Just think if he could see her now!

'I can't stay,' she said to Henny, who was pregnant again and looked warm and happy around her eyes. 'I just popped in, and since he was sleeping, I thought –'

'Fine, fine,' said Henny. 'Now you just sit right down there. Relax, dear. Take a break.'

And the room was so bright; it was the sunshine. There was a sewing machine, and there were clothes everywhere, and she really didn't know why, but she started crying. Then she blew her nose with an awful blast; then she started laughing and couldn't stop.

'Ow,' she said, 'my belly hurts. You know, you're right, Henny. It's in my belly. It's bubbling right up.'

And Henny actually had tears in her eyes too. Henny went over and put her arms around her, and some of the icy crust melted, and it was soft and bright inside her for a moment, and she would remember that for the rest of her life. She had never felt anything like it. She was only visiting her sister, whose husband she couldn't stand because there was so much noise and laughter around him.

'Now listen,' said Henny, 'you can't keep going on like this. He's got you frightened out of your wits. Don't you think we see what's happening?'

'But,' she said, at a loss for words. She was offended, and she had to go home. 'Sweet Henny,' she said, 'what do you mean? I'm just a bit tense. He doesn't do anything to me. It's just that night job. Poor thing, he has a hard time sleeping during the day. And if I only had a cat –'

Now she was talking nonsense. She really shouldn't mix a

cat up with this appalling accusation. She should put Henny in her place, and yet she said it anyway, as if Henny hadn't said any of that rubbish:

'Just a little cat, a soft, warm kitten, purring quietly. It could lie in my lap and purr all day long, Henny. Do you think you can get me a cat?'

'Have you asked him?'

'No, but I was just about to today. I'm going home to ask him right now. You mustn't think I'm afraid of him.'

She stopped talking. Her eyes surveyed the room. Then her attention went inward. He was awake. She could feel it through the walls and buildings, through the oceans, through three years of strained attentiveness. She flapped her arms a little to get up from the chair more quickly. The sun blinded her. She longed to sit at the table and listen to the ceiling. She longed for the sound of the bed creaking. She couldn't stand being away from that sound. Her heart was pounding wildly.

'Sorry,' she said to Henny, and, 'Goodbye, kids,' to the indistinct small people dancing around in the sun's rays. And Henny shouted something after her, but the wind blew it off course.

'Okay,' she shouted back, 'okay.'

Let it go well, just this once, she thought, and, as God is my witness I will never ask for a cat, just let him be asleep. Just don't let him be awake.

She removed her shoes outside on the mat, and crept in sideways through the door, as if it would make less noise if it weren't opened so wide. Then she stood, stiff as a statue in the door to the living room, because there he sat, with the newspaper open in front of him, leaning forward toward his cup of coffee. Incredibly slowly, he lifted his head, and he looked her up and down as if he had never seen her before.

'Well,' he said flatly, 'has something horrible happened? You look like it.'

'No.'

She took one step toward him, then stood still again.

'I – I just stopped in at Henny's. I figured since you were sleeping –'

Her voice receded and cracked.

'I heard you leave,' he said, engrossed again in the newspaper.

She stared at his Adam's apple. It was going up and down, up and down. If only it would stop. If only something would stop. She would feel better if he would calm down his Adam's apple.

'I would like to – I mean – don't you think it would be nice to have a little cat?'

'They smell,' he said, irritated. 'You shouldn't let her put nonsense like that in your head.'

'No.' She hung her jacket in the closet.

Then she sat down carefully in her usual chair, taking pains to take up as little room as possible. He read the ads. His face was horrible. Worse than when there were typos, she thought. She shouldn't have gone. By constantly staying home, she warded off something terrible that was always just about to happen, something she was expecting, something that she, every day, minute by minute, pushed back into place like a wall that would topple if you didn't press against it with all your might.

The clock struck six.

He neatly folded the newspaper and observed her silently for a moment.

He said slowly, 'There were no typos.'

'Oh, thank goodness,' she said, 'thank goodness! Then

forget about that thing with the cat, Arthur. It doesn't matter. They do smell terrible. You're absolutely right. I'll go and put the potatoes on to boil.'

And she skipped out of the room, smiling vacantly, while making small, defensive hand gestures in the air, as if she were swatting at invisible flies.

She didn't dare think what would have happened if there had been typos in the paper too.

The Mother

'Rubbish!' she said, 'Trivialities! Don't waste your time. The handkerchiefs are here; the shirts are in the drawer to the right. That's everything. Pay attention to what's important.'

She loved straight lines, smooth surfaces, flush doors. She hated coffered ceilings and drifting conversation. In the mornings she was up before everyone else. She walked through the rooms with her clacking wooden heels, removing flowers that were taking too long to wilt.

They lay in their narrow, coffin-like beds listening to her footsteps. She never woke them. She didn't involve herself in their lives. But they had to interrupt her. At certain intervals they had to ask about the handkerchiefs and the shirts. They had to hear her say the same short, imposing phrases again and again. *Rubbish! Trivialities!* They stared, helplessly fascinated by her sharp, hawkish nose, her bulldog jaw, and her clear, sunken eyes which constantly narrowed and cut to the heart of the matter. They followed her from the curved alcoves in which they had hidden themselves, as she thumbed through bills, calculated, balanced the budget, or called the butcher to order large, thick slabs of meat to fry or boil. She sat erect at the table, eating quickly and impatiently, for no particular reason, and everyone hurried to finish at the same time as her.

In the evening she retired to her room to tear up old letters and red silk ribbons, and in the morning the waste basket was filled to the top. When he entered her room, she was smoothing out her sheet. She couldn't sleep with the least wrinkle underneath her. He said: 'Maybe we ought to – I mean, life is short, and sometimes I dream your name is Leonora.'

She squeezed her eyes shut and offered him her dry, wrinkle-free cheek. 'Yes,' she said, 'that is part of it. That is perfectly all right.'

She didn't get involved. But they knew everything would fall apart if she left for a single day, for even an hour. Then they would get totally lost among these long, dark hallways, these floor-to-ceiling mirrors, these useless stucco angels, these piles of dying flowers and flapping silk ribbons, stolen by little boys from the cemetery's stiff wreaths – these soft, powder-blue beds with decorative pictures adhered to the headboards, these loving, seaweed-covered arms, reaching out for them everywhere, this sweet, suffocating smell of decomposition and incense.

'The essentials,' she said, and she was right. 'Whatever is sensible, smooth, straight, or flat.'

When he wasn't disturbing her, she read. She was fond of verse that rhymed properly and of highly condensed, cramped text in small books, where the pages were utilized fully and economically by certain essayists, philosophers, and memoirists who understood the rare art of keeping to the point. She detested novels and short stories. They were a waste of time. They kept people from real life. They were meandering and uneven. Rubbish!

When she was reading, it was totally quiet in the house. Sometimes she appeared in the hall, and they emerged from the doorways of their rooms, breathless with listening and lurking.

'Young people need to enjoy themselves,' she said. 'They have to get it over with before it's too late.'

Then they got their shirts and handkerchiefs and went out to enjoy themselves, with their aging, dispirited faces. She never asked where they had been or when they got back. 'Other mothers,' she said. They guiltily swallowed the large pieces of meat, ashamed of their clean nails with their bright, white half-moons, embarrassed by their smooth-shaven chins.

She showed him the household budget. 'The butcher, the baker, the grocer,' she said, stabbing a broad, dry, squarish nail down on each soundless entry. 'Okay,' he said quickly, blushing. 'It's not really necessary –'

'Oh, yes,' she said with her smooth, flat abdomen at the same height as his nose. 'It must be done. We have to get it over with.'

'Mother,' they said.

Then they fell silent again under her inquisitive look, because there was never anything essential they needed her for, no topic of a concrete nature which they could lay out quickly and precisely. Then they said, 'Where are the shirts? Where are the handkerchiefs?' Her response calmed them. For a moment it cleared the burden of guilt from their hearts, making it less difficult to breathe. And they stared at her constantly from their secret corners, from their storm-swept tower chambers, from the horrible crookedness of their souls, trapdoors, and unsmoothable wrinkles. 'Rubbish!' she said. 'Trivialities! Get to the point!'

'Grow up,' she said.

And all their lives they stood listening, anxiety-ridden, not far from her, while in the evening she tore apart silk ribbons and letters. There was no end to it, and they never gave a thought to who emptied the waste basket and took out the garbage. It was completely inessential. Maybe it was their wives, maybe a housekeeper –

A Fine Business

The real estate agent stopped his car outside the apartment complex where the young couple lived. They were going with him to look at houses. With a broad smile he opened the car door and let them in. He thought they were both very nice. The husband was in his early thirties; his face suggested a firm character and the ability to get ahead in the world. The wife, who was very pregnant, didn't say much. She seemed to be floating on a pink cloud of infatuation and was full of submissive wonder at anything to do with this business, which she didn't understand at all. An easy couple. An inheritance had fallen into their laps, the size of which he was well aware. In general – he started the car – people who didn't make waves. The man was evidently rather particular, but the agent liked young people who had their heads on straight.

'We'll drive to Bregnerød today,' he said. 'I have something there that will be just the thing for you. Four rooms, a den, central heating, and a charming yard. Don't pay attention to the fact it seems a bit empty. The wife is divorced and has to sell quickly. All she cares about is the down payment.'

'How much does she want?' asked the husband, who also cared only about the down payment.

'Twenty-five thousand.' He tapped the ash from his cigar. 'But she'll go lower.'

'Does she have children?' asked the wife, leaning her head against her husband's shoulder while turning one of the buttons on his coat.

'You can say that again.'

The agent gave a resounding laugh.

'Three of them. One still in a crib.'

'Is the furnace good?' asked the husband. He was learning about the vulnerable parts of a house.

'Everything's first class. The husband just ran off.'

'Oh,' she cried sympathetically, 'from three children!'

She glanced up at her husband. He would never do that, she thought. The child inside her moved, and her oval face took on a sweet, trance-like expression.

Her husband determined, with a certain distaste, that the real estate agent's collar was sprinkled with gray dandruff. When he advanced to a higher position in his company, he would pay attention to little things like that, and people with top-notch references wouldn't understand why they had been passed over. The thought appealed to him.

The car slipped out of the city, through the suburban housing developments. She smiled at the children playing. In less than a month she would be adjusting her baby carriage on a lawn, so the sun wouldn't shine on the little one's face. Her yard. Her baby. They would have to make up their minds soon.

'I hope you like this house,' she said.

He patted her distractedly on the hand. Recently he had been studying the fine details of purchasing real estate. No one was going to fool him with a dolled-up money pit. They had seen quite a few of those recently.

'How much lower do you think she'll go?' he asked, leaning forward toward the agent's thick neck.

'I would say four to five thousand. Women in her situation are desperate for cash.'

'She really wants to sell?'

He lit a cigarette and squeezed his eyes shut to avoid the smoke.

The real estate agent gave his resounding laugh again, which ended in a coughing fit.

'You can bet on it. She doesn't have two pennies to rub together.'

'You're not thinking of cheating her, are you?' asked the wife with a worried voice.

'Leave the business to us,' said her husband, giving her a tender, paternal look. 'We're talking about our future.' Then he added, more softly, 'And the baby's.'

The house was located in a small town. They drove past the bar and the church, which were right next to one another, and the two men exchanged the usual jokes in that vein. She looked a bit uneasily from the one to the other. It was as if an unspoken understanding had arisen between them on account of the woman who had to sell her house. And what if we don't like it? she thought, feeling anxious. What if no one wants to buy it?

'So here we are.'

The real estate agent took her elbow chivalrously to help her out of the car. Recently she hadn't been able to tolerate anyone but her husband touching her, not even women. She only left the apartment when absolutely necessary.

'Ah, how lovely!' she exclaimed at the sight of the little red house with blue shutters and a proper iron fence around a yard, manicured and cared for by skilled hands.

With a little poke in her side, her husband reminded her about his warning against any show of excitement. She blushed a little. It wasn't easy for her to hide her feelings.

Halfway down the front walk their little parade was stopped by a boy of eight or nine with a defiant face. He stood there with his legs spread apart like a man, a vertical wrinkle between his eyebrows.

'Mommy has changed her mind,' he said in a sinister tone, looking at the real estate agent, who apparently knew him. 'She's decided not to sell the house.'

The real estate agent laughed good-naturedly and took out his wallet.

'Looks to me like you need an ice cream,' he said. 'Here you go; now get going.'

The boy flipped the coin up in the air with a studied effortlessness and caught it again. He strode off without a word of thanks.

'Don't worry about him,' said the real estate agent, tossing his cigar into a forsythia hedge. 'That's just something he made up.'

She watched the boy go. He wasn't wearing socks. It was the beginning of May, and it was cold.

Smiling uneasily at the agent, the woman opened the door and invited them in with a vague hand gesture. She was somewhere between thirty and forty years old. Her face was quite pretty, but her hair was dull and unkempt. She was wearing an apron with a wet spot, as if she had just come from the sink. A little girl of five or six stood beside her, pulling on her dress while observing the strangers with a cross face. With visible, strained effort, the real estate agent patted her on the cheek. He didn't have any children himself. The girl twisted shyly away from his large hand.

'Well!' He rubbed his hands together. 'Sorry we're arriving without notice, but I didn't know your phone had been cut off. I tried calling you.'

'I forgot to pay it,' the mother said quickly, untying her apron. 'Please, come in.'

She led them from the entry into a large living room which was separated from a bedroom by a glass door. From the other side they could hear the persistent cries of an infant.

She looked toward the door.

'I was just about to nurse,' she said apologetically. 'It can wait a little. Here is the family room,' she said, with a watchful glance at the potential buyers. 'Excuse the mess –'

'That doesn't matter,' said the wife, looking around.

There were sharply defined areas on the floor from furniture that had recently been removed. On the faded walls, the original color was revealed in small squares. The few remaining pieces of furniture were collected in the center of the floor in a kind of 'guests visiting' composition, hastily and temporarily arranged. The sun streamed in diagonally over the windowsill, where the soil in the potted plants was so dry it was full of cracks.

The wife felt a chill and pulled her jacket more tightly around her throat.

'This is very roomy,' she said, peering inquisitively up at her husband.

He could try and look a little friendlier, she thought.

He stared up at the ceiling and pointed at a dark spot.

'Does the roof leak?' he asked skeptically.

The real estate agent shrugged his shoulders.

'Minor problem,' he said. 'A roof tile is broken. It will just cost a few kroner to have it repaired.'

'Those kinds of things ought to have been taken care of.'

The young man regarded the house's owner coolly. Her baby's crying had changed to a resigned whimper.

'You can go ahead and nurse if you want,' said the wife quickly. 'Mr Henriksen can show us around while you're busy.'

She was getting tired of standing. It's a good thing he notices things like that, she thought, trying to expunge the sad feeling nestled inside her. People who sell houses always hide the flaws.

Her husband looked at her, and his eyes took on a softer expression.

'Why don't you sit down, Grete?' he said, and his instinctive contempt for the other woman was now bolstered by something concrete. As a mother she ought to know that you at least offer a pregnant woman a chair.

The real estate agent laughed again. It rumbled from his belly like an empty barrel bouncing down an incline. He observed Grete delicately as she sat down.

'Men will be men,' he stated rather hollowly, shaking his head with regret. 'Shall we go upstairs? Go ahead and nurse, ma'am. I can take care of this.'

The woman hesitated, as if she lacked confidence that he could 'take care of this' to her satisfaction. The little girl's clear voice suddenly filled the brief pause that followed. She was standing gripping a corner of her mother's dress.

'When it rains, it splashes down through the ceiling.'

The mother shook her dress free. Irritated, she blushed.

'Keep your mouth shut,' she threatened.

The child put her arm in front of her face as if she were

expecting to get hit. She had the same defiant expression on her face that her brother had had not long before.

The real estate agent was about to die of laughter.

'If you're not careful, your kids will chase all the buyers away,' he said. And then the joviality disappeared instantly from his face, as if an invisible hand had erased it. Grete suddenly saw a glimmer in his eye, which gave her an anxious feeling. She smiled at the girl, who did not smile back.

'Oh, you must be sorry to be leaving your house,' she said in a friendly voice. 'That's only natural.'

The real estate agent nodded and cut the tip off a new cigar.

'Children don't know what's good for them.'

He looked knowingly at the mother as if he were waiting for her to agree with him.

The husband wrinkled his brow.

'Is it true it leaks when it rains?' he asked in an interrogatory tone.

The woman blushed slowly all the way down to her throat like a child who is caught in a lie. She opened her mouth to respond, but the real estate agent beat her to it.

'Nonsense,' he said flatly.

His body language still exuded all the predictable cheer that the profession demanded, but Grete noticed again a warning or threatening expression in his pale eyes. That hadn't been there before when they had been out house-shopping with him. She didn't understand the looks he was exchanging with the woman. She appeared as if she was afraid of him. She had her arms crossed over her chest in a kind of defensive posture.

The real estate agent took a step toward the entry.

'How about we go upstairs,' he said, changing the subject,

'so the ladies can talk. Your wife is probably too tired for the steps.'

The mother remained standing in the middle of the floor, lost and indecisive, watching the men go, as if she would have preferred to have gone with them. Then her gaze shifted to Grete's heavy form, as if she were just seeing her for the first time.

'There is something about that real estate agent I don't like,' she said crossly, unbuttoning her dress. 'If you only knew what a woman in my position goes through,' she added bitterly.

Grete looked sadly at her.

'I – I'm sorry,' she said uneasily, and suddenly it wasn't the woman or her children she felt bad for. It was something else. And it was already on its way. They had been making plans for a long time about the house their baby was going to be raised in, and there was nothing wrong with that. They had seen quite a few houses with the agent – pretty, well-maintained houses with pretty, well-maintained people inside – and it didn't seem as though it mattered much if the houses got sold or not. And both men had spoken politely and properly with the owners. She liked almost all the houses, but there was always something about them her husband didn't like. And each time that he decided they weren't going to buy it, he acted so satisfied, as if he had landed a good deal, even though they hadn't made any deal at all. Why had he looked that way at the little stain on the ceiling? It was the same way he looked at the woman and the little girl, almost as if they too were defects in the house that could drive down the price. He probably wasn't going to buy this house either. And when they got home, he would act as if he had made the most ingenious deal in his life. She was getting so tired of house-hunting, owning them a little in her mind, and then losing them again. She had a horrible feeling they would never buy a house, and suddenly she was on the verge of tears.

'Do you want to see the baby?'

The woman got up, and her face took on a softer expression. The little girl had sat down to play at a toy kitchen in a corner of the room. They could hear the men's footsteps through the ceiling.

She held the infant in her arms and looked proudly at Grete.

'Isn't he adorable?' she asked while she sat down and put her nipple in the baby's mouth.

'He certainly is.'

Grete observed curiously the wrinkled little head which was bald at the back, like all babies. She smiled.

'I'm looking forward to having mine,' she said confidentially.

A shadow fell across the mother's face.

'We had been married eleven years,' she said into the air. 'Then my husband met a young woman at the office –'

She lifted her gaze and looked Grete in the eye.

'I still don't understand it,' she said. 'That he really is never coming back. And leaving me to take care of everything. He said, "Just sell the house, then you'll have that money." And he knows I have no sense for things like this. You don't even know the person you're married to.'

Grete bowed her head as if from an invisible blow.

'No,' she said quietly, and she felt anguish in her heart. She longed to go home.

The men came down the stairs. In the entry they engaged in animated whispering. Then they appeared in the doorway. The real estate agent was puffing heavily on his cigar.

'Isn't it true,' he said, looking at the mother, 'that you are willing to go down to twenty thousand?'

'In cold, hard cash,' he added, when she didn't answer. 'And the apartment is a good one – two rooms and a den. Cheap.'

It was an exchange.

The husband leaned against the door jamb and sized up the room's dimensions.

She looked up and made a reflexive gesture to cover her breast. Lots of thoughts swirled in her head. You couldn't trust anyone. The real estate agent was going to get one percent of the price, so he was only interested in closing the deal. He didn't care about the down payment. He didn't like her. What had she done to him? If only the kids hadn't gone and said those things. That was embarrassing. But they didn't understand. They didn't want to leave the house. They had grown up in it. They had friends on the street. They didn't have socks. The grocer's bill was growing; the stores were starting to complain. They all stared at her with the same expression as the men in the house. Countless people had stomped around her rooms and still wouldn't buy. Hopefully her son wouldn't come running in to tell them how the sewer system backed up regularly and flooded the cellar. Twenty thousand was still a lot of money. She was exhausted. She had been abandoned by one man and was dependent on other men, who looked at her as if she were an invalid, as if they could sense why he had left. And the children were misbehaving. Sometimes they looked at her the same way.

She sighed deeply and stood up with the baby in her arms.

'If you think it's reasonable,' she said.

The real estate agent's face was hidden in a smoky fog. She bent over the crib, tucking the comforter around the infant.

The two men winked at one another behind her back. Grete cast her eyes down and carefully straightened a crease in her dress. There was a charged atmosphere in the room.

'But you know I was expecting twenty-five thousand.'

The mother stood up and, with the back of her hand, brushed the hair from her forehead. She looked at the pregnant wife as if making a plea, but the younger woman looked away, as if meeting her gaze was dangerous. Her ears were buzzing. He had decided! She didn't have to walk around in strange houses anymore on the heels of this agent she couldn't stand. Why did Ejnar go along with cheating the poor woman? They had planned on putting down twenty-five thousand the whole time. But maybe they weren't cheating her. They were men; they understood business transactions. This could be nice, when it was painted and fixed up. Would the woman and her three children like their little apartment? Her heart was beating fast. 'You don't even know the person you're married to.' That was a strange thing to say to her. What was true for one person wasn't necessarily true for other people.

'That was the agreement,' said the woman dispiritedly. 'It's hard to know what to say, when I don't have anyone to talk it over with.'

The real estate agent rubbed his hands together as if he were about to dive into a pool of ice-cold water.

'That's why I'm here,' he said. 'I'm only thinking of your benefit.'

He shrugged his shoulders apologetically.

'The young couple can't afford any more than that.'

'Right, I see,' she said softly. 'Then I guess I'll have to go along with it.'

The agent took the cigar from his mouth and suddenly became lively and efficient. He asked everyone to sit around the table in the middle of the room, and he pulled papers out of his folder.

'You sign here.'

He gave the young man a fountain pen, and they spoke in a businesslike manner, almost with elation. Words like priority, appraised value, and mortgage floated in the air around the two silent women who each sat lost in her own thoughts.

When everything was in order, the real estate agent regarded the nice young couple with a satisfied expression. Happy people, he thought, with a pleasant, albeit vague sensation of having played the role of their benefactor. The husband got up quickly. He thought the air was bad. Grete looked pale.

'Goodbye. Nice doing business with you,' he said rather formally, shaking the owner's hand. 'I will send you the check tomorrow.'

Grete tried to say goodbye to the little girl sitting on the floor in front of her play kitchen, but she glared up at her crossly and put both her hands behind her back.

Grete turned around self-consciously. She would have liked to see what the upstairs was like, but the men seemed to be in a hurry to leave.

Out in the yard they stopped and looked at the house again.

He put his arm around his wife's shoulders.

'Well,' he said gently, 'Are you happy? That was a good deal, you can trust me on that.'

She looked down and scraped the ground with the tip of her shoe.

'Why didn't you give her what she was asking?' she asked. 'We have the money.'

Both men laughed heartily.

'Women,' said the real estate agent condescendingly.

The sun was going down. Shadows fell across the brick wall. A sudden nausea rose inside her. She leaned against her husband.

'It's a good thing you can think for both of us,' she said.

'For all three of us,' he smiled, correcting her.

The real estate agent tilted his head like an affectionate bird.

'Young people,' he said, feeling moved.

Then he laughed his peculiar, gratuitous laughter, which rolled down the front walk like a partly deflated ball.

The three of them walked to the car.

From behind the curtain, the mother stood watching them leave.

The Bird

She had the taxi stop outside the senior housing and asked the driver to wait a moment. It wasn't long before she came out with her mother and helped her into the car. She said the name of the hospital. It was rather far away.

'There's really no reason for it,' said her mother passively with a sigh. 'I was just thinking, when I called you, that maybe Asger would have time to drive me out there.'

'He's working a lot of overtime at the office.'

Vera could hear the unfriendly edge in her own voice, so she added, in a gentler tone:

'We're both busy. The pre-school teaching assistant is sick. But maybe he'll be feeling better today.'

'That would be nice, but I doubt it,' said her mother.

Her entire life she always expected the worst.

The glare from a streetlight briefly lit her mother's face. Her hat was askew on her white hair, and her head trembled continuously, but subtly. Vera knew it was sclerosis. Her mother called it *nerves*.

'Villy was really startled when he saw his father yesterday,' she said.

Her voice sounded slightly triumphant.

'Afterward he said he had never seen him so low. Both he and Asta are so nice about driving me there. But they were invited out tonight, so they couldn't do it.'

Asta was Vera's sister-in-law, Villy's third wife. Vera had been married three times too. But this time, she thought, Villy had gotten lucky. Asta was a sweet person, and she adored him.

'You know I don't have a driver's license,' Vera said in a tired voice. 'And Ole gets so upset when I go out in the evening.'

Ole was her youngest, a late arrival, now seven years old.

'I understand very well,' muttered her mother. 'But I didn't mean for you to hire a taxi.'

'It doesn't matter,' Vera forced herself to say.

She was sweating. Why in the world did they place him in the city's most distant hospital? And on top of that, why couldn't she take her mother's hand and comfort her? They were in separate corners of the back seat; only their jackets were touching. Villy did things like that. Put his arm around her shoulder, got her to laugh. Villy always was the pride of the family. He had been such a bright, good-looking child. He got his lively, youthful bearing from his mother. When they were children, the two of them shared a buoyancy which she and her father were not a part of. They were each on their own. Vera couldn't remember ever having had a real conversation with her father. When she was grown up enough, and it became possible, he was already going deaf. And besides, what would they have talked about? He was forty years older than her; in her eyes he had always been an old man. She had shared their bedroom for the fourteen years of her life that she lived at home, and she had been witness to such an impoverished, pitiful married life that she didn't understand how they still couldn't live without one another. God in heaven how they fought! And how the poor man always had to give in. It might have been smarter to marry a man ten years older. Then maybe it would have been possible to hold onto him. All Vera's husbands had been younger –

'We haven't seen Asger in a long time,' said her mother from her side of the seat. 'He isn't sick, is he?'

Vera's heart beat faster. The old childhood anxiety crept through her. She could feel her mother's scrutinizing gaze.

'God, no,' she answered quickly, 'he's perfectly fine. It's just some salary negotiations. They take up all his time.'

You just had to blurt out some terms she didn't understand.

'You can imagine how Ruffy misses her Daddy,' said her mother in a confidential tone. 'I had to baby her all afternoon.'

Ruffy was their parakeet. They had had several. They always named them Ruffy and they were always – to her father's dismay – sold or put down when they reached the age at which they 'sat and scratched', as her mother put it with disgust.

'Now try and look happy, Mother,' she said, as they walked down the long hospital corridor. 'It will cheer up Dad.'

For herself she adopted the attitude she used for parents of difficult children. She really did feel bad for the old man, and she had every reason to wish him back to health. Besides, it cost her about forty kroner to drive her mother back and forth. And lately she had had to pay attention to money.

He lay with his weathered, sunken face turned toward the door, and there was a prick in Vera's heart when she saw him. It was as if he had grown smaller since last week. Her most recent visit had been the day after the operation, and since then his skin had turned yellowish. The whites of his eyes were yellowed too. But he smiled genuinely as he kissed his wife on both cheeks. When that was over, he noticed Vera. She patted him awkwardly on the cheek.

'Hi Dad,' she shouted. 'You look fresh.'

'What'd you say?'

She shouted it even louder, and he rose up on his elbow with a painful grimace.

'I feel pretty good,' he said. 'I'm thinking I can go home in a couple of days.'

His breathing was fast, and her mother sank down in a chair, observing him with a deeply concerned expression. She looked up at the board over his bed.

'He's in a bad way,' she said to Vera. 'His pulse is all the way up to eighty.'

'That's totally normal,' she answered, irritated. 'He doesn't even have a fever.'

When she couldn't find anything to say to him, Vera just smiled cheerfully. It was a shared room. In the other bed lay a man with his mouth open, his gaze directed stiffly at the ceiling. Her mother had said he almost always looked like that. He had come from a mental hospital and would be going back. No one ever came to visit him.

Her father lay back down on his pillow. They had removed a tumor from his hip. The doctors had told Villy it was benign. But they probably always said that to the family. The operation had gone well, they said, considering his advanced age.

'How did you get here?' he asked in a weak voice.

'Taxi,' yelled her mother in his ear. 'I told Vera it was too expensive, but Asger didn't have time to drive us, and you know how I feel about trolleys.'

'Right,' he whispered, glancing somewhat reproachfully at Vera, who stood leaning in, at the foot of the bed.

'Your mother gets all confused,' he said a bit louder and

with obvious effort. 'She can't find her way around town at night. The trolleys drive her crazy.'

'Well, thank goodness for Villy and Asta,' said her mother, taking off her hat. Her head started to tremble more, as if its stabilizer had been removed.

It was hot, and Vera unbuttoned her coat. How was she going to avoid having to invite her mother in for a cup of coffee when they got back? Last time, Villy had taken care of it. Her mother couldn't stand being alone. She didn't go to bed until the middle of the night and she slept with the light on.

The old man dozed off. His lips were pulled back from the black stumps of his teeth, which didn't meet anymore. His chest whistled laboriously.

'Oh, God.' Her mother dried her eyes behind her glasses. 'He's not going to make it, Vera! Can't you see how yellow he looks!'

'A little jaundice is normal,' she said, not caring whether the statement was true or not. 'Don't show him how hard it is on you. Tell him something to cheer him up. Something about the bird.'

He opened his eyes without realizing he had been asleep.

'Ruffy misses you,' said her mother with clear mouth movements. 'She's become very unsettled. She misses being able to peck at your beard.'

A smile brightened his shrunken face.

'Yes,' he said, 'that is one smart bird. We're going to keep her, aren't we?'

Her mother's mouth went sour.

'Only till she gets old,' she said. 'You know that very well.'

When she saw how downhearted her answer made him, she put her mouth back to his ear.

'Emmy's daughter is getting divorced,' she yelled trium-phantly. 'Her husband already has someone else.'

'Well,' he mumbled, satisfied. 'She is, is she? Then she can come down off her high horse.'

Emmy was Vera's cousin, a daughter of her mother's sister. When Villy and Vera got divorced from their spouses, the aunt had bragged that something scandalous like that would never happen to her Emmy. The two sisters had always tried to outdo one another. Emmy's mother had secured for herself a skilled laborer as a husband while the younger sister had to be satisfied with an unskilled laborer. Then it was about the children. Emmy married a reliable craftsman, while Vera and Villy had risen socially. But then the divorces happened, which were impossible to hide. Maybe Emmy hadn't risen up the social ladder, but at least she would never get divorced. She had always been such a nice girl.

Vera hadn't seen Emmy since they were children. And she had forgotten that she had a daughter.

'Right, that's what I always said to Amanda,' yelled her mother. 'No one is immune!'

Sister Amanda was eighty-six.

Vera felt exhausted. The sharp hospital smell was giving her nausea. Having visiting hours only in the evening was so impractical. How in the world was she going to get her mother to go directly home?

The nurse came in and straightened both patients' pillows.

'Visiting hours are over,' she said quietly.

Just at that moment Villy walked in the door, broad and solid, dressed up as for a party, and with beads of rain in his black hair. Vera flushed with joy and relief. Villy had also thought about the problem. He would see to it.

'Greetings, everyone,' he said in his resonant voice. 'Hello, Dad, you look great.'

He shook his father's limp hand and blinked a couple of times when he saw how sluggish he was. Then he turned toward his mother and kissed her dutifully on the cheek. Over her shoulder he flashed a comforting smile to Vera.

'Hi, little sister,' he said.

He took both her hands in his.

'I'll drive you home,' he said cheerfully. 'You first, then Mother.'

Although he said it very casually, a charged mood immediately spread between them and their mother. The only sound was their father's wheezing breaths. He was asleep again. Out in the hall, visitors filed past.

Their mother put on her hat with an insulted look on her face.

'I would have liked to have stopped in and seen Asger and the children,' she said. 'I don't need to rush home to those empty rooms.'

'Well, of course,' boomed Villy, for a second resembling a little boy, despite his nearly fifty years. 'It's just that I have to get back to the others. I left right in the middle of things –'

He scratched his head and avoided Vera's eyes.

'Mother has to go home to the parakeet. It would be a pity otherwise. Ruffy isn't used to being left alone.'

The three of them turned and looked at the man in the bed, as if they had nearly forgotten him. He returned their disconcerted stares with a faint hint of the strength he could have mustered in a long forgotten time, when faced with something completely trivial. Then he shut his eyes again, and the wheezing in his chest continued. The stream of visitors was ebbing away, and the nurse appeared again in the door.

'Visiting hours are *over*,' she said sharply.

'Fine, fine,' said their mother pitifully, and her head shook more than usual.

'I'll go along – since Villy wants it that way – who knows how long he'll be with us –'

She stuck her hand under her powerful son's helpful bent arm, and he looked back at Vera as they made their way to the elevator.

They smiled at one another, relieved.

The Little Shoes

Helene woke early in the morning, feeling that her entire life was one big failure. She had lost control over it. She attributed this paralyzing and depressing state to a variety of totally different causes, like when an animal gets caught in a trap and searches for a way out first in one corner, then in another. But every day ended with one convincing reason – the only convincing reason she had – namely, that she had absolutely no control over her surroundings, and that it wasn't in her power to change anything about her life, or to change the people who had made it a failure.

Her husband coughed in the next room, and his bed creaked as he turned over. She pondered how they once had been happy together, how they used to love one another. It had been over six months since he had held her in his arms, and that last embrace had been different from all the others. Now she thought even that evening it had been obvious, it had been a kind of goodbye. It was as if with all his strength, but in vain, he had tried to force the old feelings to appear, and afterward he had looked at her for a long time with a mute, reproachful stare.

Helene felt a taste like dust in her mouth, and noticed the aroma of sweat and sleep from her body. It had become as unfamiliar to her as it had to him. She couldn't stand herself when others couldn't either. She closed her eyes and heard Hanne's voice from the kitchen. She was sitting drinking coffee with the children, fresh and in good moods, while the record player from her son's bedroom babbled some vacuous pop melody. All day long there was a cacophony around this difficult young woman, whom Helene was constantly on the brink of firing, though it hadn't amounted to anything yet. She told herself it didn't really matter, which had no effect as she lay there curled up under her comforter, dully angered by the girl's existence. When she complained about Hanne, her husband laughed and said that she should look at it from a comedic point of view. 'Hanne isn't a person,' he declared jovially, 'she's a phenomenon.' He was in such a good mood lately, so upbeat and busy with his work. Helene wasn't working anymore. She was a child psychologist and had enjoyed her job in a psychiatric ward, but then their life had been turned upside down when Henrik explained to her that it would be a tax advantage if she stopped working. It now felt like a big mistake to have given in to his irrefutable arguments. All day long, all she could do was nurse her despondency. She couldn't even gather herself to read. She wasn't interested in the company of her friends anymore. It was as if a zone of loneliness had appeared around her, and perhaps somehow she had created it herself.

It was eight o'clock, and Hanne was expecting her to get out of bed after the kids were off to school, so she could clean. Hanne didn't waste any effort on the accommodating side of her personality. Helene was sure the girl knew she was unhappy, and maybe why as well.

Just as she put her bare feet on the cold linoleum floor, Henrik opened the door between their rooms and walked over to his side of their shared dressing closet – a monstrosity that filled an entire wall – where he started rummaging through his clean shirts without giving her as much as a glance. Still, she could tell from his back that he wanted to say something nice.

'I'm getting up now,' he said. 'You can tell Hanne. And get her to turn off that blasted record player.'

Helene felt under the bed for her shoes. Lately she had always felt slovenly or dressed wrong when he was around.

'Then she'll start singing,' she said. 'I can't cut her vocal chords.'

'No. Unfortunately.'

He laughed appreciatively, as if she had made a joke, then walked back to his room with his shirt slung over his striped pyjama shoulder. It occurred to her that they never talked about anything but Hanne, as if she were the only link between them. It seemed crazy.

She put on her old robe and walked down the long hallway to the kitchen.

'Good morning,' she said, leaning up against the door jamb. 'My husband is getting up now, so you can make coffee. And can you please turn off the record player?'

Hanne looked up at her with her narrow green eyes. She was sitting with her elbows on the table and a cup in her hands. A thick, knitted sweater accentuated her generous bosom. Helene had to fight back the impulse to fire her on the spot. She stood there until the girl slowly got up, wearing a shameless smile that radiated the consciousness of the sexual superiority of idiotic youth.

Helene took it as the kind of smile you give to an older, discarded fellow female, and she was infuriated.

On the way to the bathroom Helene stumbled over her daughter's shoes. She picked one up and examined it carefully, gently stroking the fine, red leather with her hand. It was a small shoe – size 36 – high-heeled and open, with a short, flared upper; a somewhat affected, coquettish shoe, which looked good for nothing except making you wiggle, though Linda could walk in them with no problem. The thought of eighteen-year-old Linda was a haven in Helene's homeless heart, and as she stood there in the darkened hallway with the little feminine object in her hand, a tenderness for her first-born spread like a balm over her plagued consciousness. Henrik loved and coddled Linda, just as she herself always had. As stepfather, he acted according to plan. He loved the girl, and tried heroically to hide his antipathy toward the boy. The children had been seven and four when they had married. Her first husband had died of tuberculosis. The tragedy of it never really penetrated her, and only through great effort could she recall the circumstances with any detail. To her the past never seemed real.

'May I shave now?' asked Henrik politely, and it startled her. She hadn't heard him coming.

'Of course,' she said, confused, and it seemed to her that he looked from the little shoe in her hand down to her own squarish, flat house shoes – size 39 – out of which her feet, which were always a little swollen in the morning, stuck out in an old-womanish, unsightly way. It lasted just a second, then he disappeared into the bathroom, and she told herself she was overreacting, which didn't prevent the meaningless episode from ruining her fragile good mood.

She wandered into the dining room and sat down, feeling miserable, at the large conference-sized table, which Hanne was setting with superfluous movements and superfluous noise. Helene was able to assume an expression which prevented conversation. Whatever Hanne said caused her anxiety and alarm, for reasons she couldn't pin down. She just wasn't meant to have help around the house. She wasn't meant to be taken care of and grow dependent on others. And over and above that, she wasn't meant to be forty and have nearly grown children. Hanne was the result of two fateful events in her family. The first was Henrik's promotion at work, to a highly responsible position incompatible with their previously modest lifestyle. This position, the detailed duties of which Helene didn't know, required a more elegant home. Through Henrik's connections they got a seven-room apartment in the center of Copenhagen, sold their little house, got an interior decorator to furnish the new apartment, and finally, hired Hanne as living proof of their social advancement. The furniture they hadn't discarded was in her room, where various young men took turns sitting and reclining on the red sofa which had decorated their previous living room. Hanne was an omnivore concerning men, and she evidently valued quantity above all. They had held two parties in the six months since they moved, and Helene had felt rather awkward in her role as hostess for Henrik's colleagues and their perfect, acerbic wives, who seemed to have intimate knowledge of their husbands' work. It was something to do with buying and selling iron. Helene's domestic skills were negligible, and Hanne had shown up in long pants with her intolerable self-inflated sense of not being the least bit inferior to others. It was possible that hiring her meant the end of their marriage.

'I was wondering,' Hanne said, leaning over her while

placing a tray of bread on the table, 'if we could collect clothes for Algiers Aid. Both Linda and Morten have lots of clothes they never wear. Linda has more shoes than she could wear out in her entire life. And Morten and I just found a pile of sweaters and socks he's outgrown. He thinks it's a great idea. He's such an unselfish boy.'

Hanne used several high-minded humanistic ideas to wage private class warfare in their family.

Why had she and Morten been collaborating on the Algiers problem? No, you couldn't affect what was going on. Hanne stood right next to her, young, and brimming with working-class resentment and self-righteousness. Helene balanced her teaspoon on the edge of her cup. She moved her chair back from the girl's imposing presence.

'Go ahead and put something together,' she said coolly.

Hanne sat down and squinted at her.

'Did you know,' she said pointedly, 'that a million people will die if they don't get help right away?'

Evidently, it was Helene's fault that a million people were going to die.

Henrik crossed the hall to get dressed, exuding the aroma of aftershave and hair gel, which reminded Helene that she needed a shower before they had breakfast together.

'Yes, I see.' She pushed out her chair and stood up. 'In the meantime take care of the coffee.'

Following an impulse, Helene opened the door to Morten's room and walked in. It was a messy boy's room with a record player, a camera and tripod, and lots of childish knick-knacks like bulky wooden swords, a pocket knife, a dusty butterfly collection on cardboard, and a homemade apparatus for chemical experiments. The walls were filled with variably executed paintings of an abstract nature, hung up with transparent tape, and the curtains, chosen by the interior decorator, had received the personal touch that comes from dirty hands. In the middle of the floor lay, as promised, a pile of discarded clothes, and Helene sat down on her son's unmade bed and stared at it. Hanne pranced by with the coffee pot, sending her a triumphant glance through the open door. She turned her head toward the window and her eye fell on an open book lying on the ink-stained desk. A strange anxiety swirled in her heart, and she walked over and picked it up. It was *Love from A–Z*, and on the inside cover was Hanne's name in clear cursive. Why in the world was she lending a book like that to a fifteen-year-old boy? He had been raised with modern values and knew plenty about those subjects. Hanne was twenty-two. Could it be . . . ?

She moved Linda's red shoes aside and, in a burst of insight, suddenly noticed that they were clean inside, that is, brand new. She couldn't bring herself to ask her husband for things that weren't absolutely necessary, but Linda could. Linda was irresistible when she stuck out her little foot and said, 'See Henrik, these can't be resoled anymore. And I saw a really pretty pair at the department store.'

He and Linda had animated conversations in the evening, sitting in the living room, her long blonde hair falling over the math problems he was helping her with. They didn't have to talk about Hanne. To Linda, Hanne simply didn't exist. One or twice in the beginning she had declined Hanne's invitations to go out with her, and Helene admired her daughter's natural distancing from this intrusive being. Linda would never have trouble with housekeepers.

While Helene got washed, she thought how it was a little strange that there had never been a young man in Linda's life, not even a boy; only a few girlfriends over for evening tea – high school girls whom Henrik gallantly drove home afterward. She was a homebody through and through, content with her books and her knitting, with a pat on the cheek in passing, with her cute girlish bedroom, which she kept spotless without Hanne's help. Morten's friends had to stay in his room, and they never got driven home. It was the way things were. Helene had always been protective of her son, and the jealousy that bubbled up between the two siblings was no more than normal.

She stared into the mirror at her greenish face. It was because of the harsh fluorescent lights which she never had the energy to change. Suddenly she thought, We should have had a child together. Exhausted, she leaned her head against the mirror, and heard Hanne singing out in the kitchen 'Tell me, why did you leave me? Please come ba-ack, Please come ba-ack . . .' From the dining room, Henrik hummed along, and Helene felt betrayed and estranged. Something was going on in the house between everyone else around her, apart from her, and right under her nose. Something which was coming closer every day. She walked to her bedroom and quickly got dressed. A button-down top and skirt. Her heart was pounding, but she took out her most uncomfortable, least clunky shoes. They were black and pointed, with a thin strap across the ankle, and curved, medium-high heels. Suddenly she had a vision of her mother. They were in a shoe store, and Helene was getting new shoes. It was shortly before she took her first job, and she was about fourteen. Her mother had said: 'This will be the last pair of shoes we buy for you.' In that moment she had seen herself through her parents' eyes as a consumer, an expense they would be free of. From that day forward she had had a troubled relationship with her mother, and she was proud of having established warmer, more lasting connections with her own children. But had she? Could you ever really know your children?

She sat across from Henrik, observing his delicate, slightly worn face and the smoke-colored circles around his eyes. It occurred to her that she didn't know him at all.

'I found a book about sex in Morten's room,' she said under her breath. 'Hanne lent it to him. I think they fool around too much, the two of them.'

Henrik laughed and took a bite of bread.

'You're just jealous,' he said. 'If she seduces him, it's only healthy. It's an old tradition that the sons of the house go to bed with the maid.'

His eyes took on a sudden snake-like expression, as if he were evaluating how much he had wounded her. He hates me, she thought, dumbfounded.

'He's only a child,' she mumbled unconvincingly.

'He's almost sixteen,' he said flatly. 'Mothers would avoid a lot of grief if they realized their children are becoming adults, even though they're still in school.'

'He might fall in love with her,' she said, confused, going silent again, because it seemed as if the conversation was about something else.

Henrik just shrugged his shoulders, stood up, and pushed his chair under the table. She got up too and stepped toward him to follow him to the entry, like she used to do back when everything between them was fine.

Perplexed, he looked down at her feet.

'Why are you wearing your dress shoes this morning?' he asked.

Then he left without waiting for an answer and without saying goodbye.

She sank down in a chair and stared out the window. The

gray November light penetrated deep inside her, lining her with stale hopelessness. Hanne came sashaying in with her affected gait and started putting cups on the tray.

'Can I take Linda's old clothes?' she said unabashedly. 'Like I said before, she'll never be able to wear out her shoes. Your husband gives her too many. If I may say so, he's a bit too infatuated with her –'

That's as far as she got.

All Helene's anxiety and despair collected into one powerful wave of anger. She saw red spots before her eyes as she slowly rose, and the girl automatically took a couple of steps back.

'You – you,' stammered Helene, 'can pack up your own old rags and leave immediately. We have no use for you anymore.'

'Good gracious.'

Hanne collected herself again immediately, and her narrow, closely set eyes were full of sinister triumph.

'I would like to receive my pay for the entire month.'

Without answering, Helene stormed into her room, flung open her desk drawer, and pulled out her checkbook. There was a small amount left from her glory days. She filled out the check with a trembling hand.

'There you go.'

She handed the check back over her shoulder to Hanne, who had followed her.

'Now go pack and leave immediately.'

Humming a tune, the intolerable person strode down the hallway to her room, and Helene kicked off her shoes, stretched her sore toes, put her head down on her desk, and sobbed.

You can't control your circumstances. You can't control

your fate. All you can do is avoid people whose words stir things up, secret things, that absolutely must not be stirred up.

With demonstrative, unrestrained noise, Hanne packed with the door open.

Feeling somewhat relieved after her bout of tears, Helene got *Love A–Z*, and handed it to the girl as if its pages were from the book of Satan.

'My son,' she said, 'will be fine without this.'

Hanne had sat down on her suitcase.

'What about Algiers Aid?' she persisted. 'You should donate the clothes – at least do it for Morten's sake. He is very concerned about it. And all Linda's shoes –'

'Leave me the address,' said Helene quickly, unable to bear hearing another word. 'I'll get it to them.'

Hanne gave her the address, and then Helene walked back through the carpeted hall, took Linda's delicate little shoes and walked across the dining room's parquet floor with them. She held them out stiffly, and when she made it into Linda's orderly room, where the ceiling was painted a tender pink hue matching the wallpaper, she let them fall to the bottom of the closet, down with the rest of them, all leaning against one another like pairs of girlfriends gossiping about incredible secrets.

The Best Joke

One morning he was sitting on the edge of the bed and he was getting divorced. His wife was standing somewhere in the room talking. Something about her mother and someone else. Home to her mother; found someone else. And at seven in the morning, when you haven't filled out your body yet and you're cold and you have to go to work. He picked his nose and didn't understand how anyone could get so ugly in five years. Maybe she wasn't ugly. Maybe she just didn't have any effect on him, the way it usually was with women. They couldn't get under his skin. She had a red bunion on her right big toe. Why did they always have to go barefoot after they got married? If he could just get her to simmer down a second so he could get away. Here he was in his tight pyjamas, sadly scratching his chin. He thought: A man in my position! She was crying and yelling and raising her hands toward the ceiling, and if she would only put on a pair of shoes, then maybe he could tell her he loved her or something like that. He could call off the divorce. But it didn't matter. It didn't matter if they were married or divorced. He had to write a speech for the boss, a toast. The book he was seeking inspiration in, before he fell asleep, was lying on his bed stand. It was called *The 1000 Best Jokes in the World.* The best joke in the world was his relationship with women. His friends would die laughing when he told them that. He had quite a few friends, and his wife didn't like any of them. They were big, noisy, happy guys, who didn't care much about women. Strange. He could never stand being with a girl for more than a couple of hours, but before she left, it was always too late. He had been married four times. He had had three children outside the marriages. The ones he didn't marry he had kids with. They didn't mean anything to him. He didn't want to see any of them. 'Children,' she sobbed, 'if at least we had had children!' It was a horrifying thought, similar to one's arms and legs suddenly starting to grow. He much preferred shrinking to expanding. First and foremost, he wasn't quick-witted. Why did women change so fast? After ten minutes, they always said he was just an overgrown boy. Then shortly afterward he would be swinging back and forth on a swing in the in-laws' yard. Such an overgrown boy, they all shouted, stuffing him, weak in the knees, into some apartment that had been there ready for him all along. And one morning an unfamiliar half-naked woman would be standing there in bare feet screaming that she wanted a divorce. That was it. His friends would enjoy this. He did too. He was a strange fellow, a tall, pathetic insect, sitting scratching his legs like a grasshopper.

'Your best friend,' she said. 'Ha, cuckold! With your best friend who you always sit with and cling to when you're drunk!' The red bunion went up and down and he lifted his gaze curiously to her face, which was just as red as the bunion. 'So it was him?' He got up and walked over to her. She was coughing like she had a fly in her throat. He was awake and fresh. 'How?' he said hoarsely. 'Where? When? Do you have any hickies? Tell me all about it, my love, tell –'

The book with the thousand jokes fell on the floor.

'Oh,' she said happily. 'You big boy! Oh –'

Two Women

When Britta was depressed, nervous, and restless like this, so not even a complete reorganization of all the furniture in the house, or the preparation of a complicated dinner, could help her, there were only two things that could alleviate her suffering: a visit to either the beauty parlor or the doctor. Sometimes both. The beauty parlor first, of course.

It was Monday, and she was the only customer. When she walked into the pretty shop, where everything, even the hair-dryers, was painted in delicate pastel colors, and the aroma of perfume and expensive soap met her like a gentle narcotic, it occurred to her that this kind of salon probably meant the same to women as bars meant to men. Just the fact that they always had artificial lighting, she thought, already feeling better, even this early in the afternoon.

No one came to help her with her overcoat, and, slightly uneasy in the silence, she hung it on one of the pink hangers in the closet herself. Then a blue figure came rushing from the back, and Britta smiled in relief when she saw that it was little Mrs Mikkelsen, who usually did her hair. But the woman didn't smile back. She seemed pale and – Britta had to fight the urge to run back out the door – her eyes were all red, as if she had been crying. This makes no sense, thought Britta, *I'm* the one with the problems. I'm the one who has been crying, not her; I'm the one with bad nerves who doesn't know a soul who understands –

She closed her eyes while her hair was washed, and she almost forgot the little hairdresser's altered demeanor under the soft, massaging fingertips caressing her scalp. It was the most soothing feeling she had ever known. She was falling asleep as she remembered one summer at the beach, the summer of her great love, long before Werner, when a young man lay next to her, playing with her hair while her fingers sifted through the warm sand, and she felt her body opening, receiving, and she was carried far away on a tide of happiness – but then suddenly the sky grew cloudy and all the beachgoers disappeared. She was all alone, and ice-cold rain started pelting her hair. She woke with a little screech:

'Aah! The water's cold! What are you doing?'

Horrified, she peered up into a face that looked just as upset as she herself felt, and she realized that there *was* something wrong, something incredible and terrible, which she, Britta, who had come here to calm her nerves, would now be unavoidably involved with for the next couple of hours. Her poor heart started pounding disconcertingly fast. She would have to mention this to the doctor – her hypersensitivity to the suffering of others. It was like a sickness. She shook her head weakly from side to side in response to the stammering apology the hairdresser mumbled, and then she shut her eyes again in resignation, as the fingers on her head pressed into a second round of shampoo lather.

Ow, unfamiliar fingers were pressing too hard, and were not evoking any more delicate, dreamy thoughts.

When she sat in front of the mirror, which reflected her face in the most flattering lighting imaginable, for some reason it made the much younger woman's face behind her look even paler, and her curiosity won out over all her other feelings.

'What's wrong, Mrs Mikkelsen?' she asked sympathetically. 'It's not like you to be so quiet. Aren't you feeling well?'

The thin pastel blue figure turned away from her, and Britta noticed with distaste that the back of the woman's hair was matted and dull.

'My husband left me yesterday – do you want me to leave it long in front of your ears, as usual?'

There was hardly a pause between the two statements, but – as Britta later explained to people when she recounted the episode – her heart nearly stopped beating at the sight of the two teardrops sliding down the young woman's cheeks.

It was too much, unfair really, that this should happen on this particular day, when she had woken in her darkest mood next to the still warm depression in the bed where Werner had slept. She wanted to laugh hysterically, because she had come here – no *rushed* here – to forget, to be soothed by vacuous but familiar and sweet chatter, to be surrounded by wonderful smells, and to be treated by caring, almost loving hands, and then –

'I feel so bad for you,' she said, and she could hear that her tone of voice, despite her efforts, was better suited to a sentence like: What does that have to do with me? Then, giving in to an irrepressible urge to be mean, she leaned in toward the mirror and added, 'Sure, just leave it as usual. My husband loves this look, I must say.'

With a nearly unnoticeable emphasis on the words: my husband.

She regretted it immediately, but at the sight of the hairdresser's slowly blushing face, she thought about Werner's
recent icy remark to her, as they were on the way out the
door to drive to the theater:

'My dear, I don't mean to insult you, but couldn't you do
your hair in a way that better matches your age?'

My God, the whole evening was ruined, even though
he immediately tried to make it up to her and blamed his
exhaustion and his work that – she didn't understand why –
had been taking up all his time. And the following days, how
did she make it through? Their kids were getting so big and
self-centered, they wouldn't understand. Irene, the eldest,
laughed to her friends: 'Please excuse my mother. She's going
through a change of life, just like us!' It was supposed to be so
incredibly funny. And what was that? Her heart! So loud she
could hear it. She couldn't stand the way it surprised her, not
unlike suddenly being shut in with this stranger who knew
everything about her. Everything! To whom she had revealed
things she wouldn't even have told her best friend. And who
had misunderstood her, misused her trust so completely, that
she thought she could proceed to trot out her own private
life! As if a person went to the salon to be entertained by the
things in life they were trying to escape from for just a little
while.

'Would you please –' she put her hand to her heart, avoiding
the other woman's eyes – 'I don't feel all that well. Would you
open a window? The air is so heavy –'

She really should visit her doctor right away. Her heart
was actually hurting. She had to bear down and not give in
to her sensitivity. She had to do that much at least for herself.
Imagine if she had told me everything, thought Britta, irritated. Why do otherwise perfectly stable people always have

a tendency to be so dramatic about it when something bad happens to them? 'My husband left me yesterday!' Unconsciously, she had never connected the little 'Mrs' in front of the woman's name with the thought of a husband.

I'd like to know, she thought, while the silent person behind her obediently opened the window and then continued pinning her curls, what Werner would think if his barber suddenly confided in him that his wife had run off! Besides, she was pretty sure that Werner never made anything but small talk with his barber. There were certain situations that only happened to her. She was too naive, too trusting.

While she sat under the dryer, and the pastel blue figure disappeared somewhere in the back, it felt like suddenly someone gave her heart a hard squeeze. She groaned loudly and shut her eyes to escape whatever horrible thing was coming, sneaking, slithering, like a crafty animal that had long been waiting, ready to ambush her. She didn't know what it was. Her thoughts jumped, terrified, away from it, but it caught up to her, condensed into one short sentence, which in a whimpering, inaudible gasp glided across her lips: I'm losing him!

But, as if some unknown being was just trying to test her stamina (there was no other way she could explain these severe mood swings), or tease her like a child with a kitten, she felt lighter as soon as she said it, or had she only thought it? Instantly she felt happier, more or less the way her friends saw her: warm, impulsive, full of interesting ideas, and always eager to drop whatever she was doing and come speeding like an ambulance as soon as anyone she knew had a problem.

She breathed deeply and smiled at her reflection. Oh, she was really going to be a beacon of good cheer as soon as she was out of here. Buy gifts for the children, for the housekeeper, prepare a nice dinner with the red wine Werner loved. Do herself up, especially her hair. Regardless of what Werner might say, just to tease her, her hair was still captivating, shiny and vibrant, blonde as sheaves of wheat, despite her forty-five years. It simply refused to grow old. And she decided, as if she had only just thought about it for the first time, to ask him flat out who that female voice was, calling on the phone last week. As soon as she heard he wasn't home, she hung up. Of course there had to be some completely natural explanation for it. She actually didn't know a single married woman who wasn't mystified by something like that once in a while. She would be insane to think – no, it was laughable.

Light in her heart, she started paging through one of the magazines that lay on the shelf under the mirror and her thoughts returned to the little hairdresser: poor girl, so young and pretty – there are plenty of men for her in the world.

She looked at her watch. She wouldn't make it to the doctor today. Why would she have gone anyway? It was probably a good thing her heart could still beat irregularly, like it did when she was a young woman.

When Mrs Mikkelsen – still silent and red-eyed, the poor thing – removed the pins and brushed out her hair, Britta smiled amiably at her in the mirror, and said in an upbeat tone:

'Don't look so unhappy, my dear. Look on the bright side. You don't have any children. If something like that happened to an old woman like me, it would be a different matter!'

She initiated a good-natured laugh which was not reciprocated.

Then she got up, relieved at being able to slip away – she would never be caught dead in here again – grabbed her purse from the counter and left a nice tip as she clasped the girl's hand around the money in a motherly fashion. Her hand was ice cold despite the heat in the shop, and Britta let go again quickly, as if she had burned herself.

'Thanks,' said the hairdresser, bowing her head slightly and following her client to the door.

'Bye, ma'am,' she said.

And, hidden behind the curtain, she watched the lady with the foolish teenage haircut leave, while unconsciously gripping the money and balling up the ten-kroner bill.

She would have liked to have had time for a good cry, but she was alone in the salon today, and the next customer was already coming in the door.

beautiful weather at the end of September.' It would help to say something like that to someone who happened to pass by. But no one came. People were sitting in their houses behind rolled-down shades, and maybe with a lit wood stove, since it was cold, and she would have said that to Mr Bruun too. There was practically no end to things like that which a person could say, and while she talked this way in a bright, upbeat voice to her children, to customers or to the morning housekeeper, she kept alive a vague uncertain hope – a child's hope, a child's anxious evening prayer: Dear God, Let everything be like before! Let my daddy come back!

Edith's eyes filled with tears, and she turned away from the deserted world to go into the house. She hadn't bought cigarettes after all. She didn't want to smoke. She had just hoped that she would meet someone, anyone she could talk to, and in whose eyes she could see herself: Edith Jørgensen, married to assistant professor Klaus Jørgensen, mother to three children, transplant to the city, but still accepted due to her friendly disposition – or was she accepted? No one really knows the impression they make on others, and likewise, Edith couldn't say what impact others had on her. It wasn't anything a person really needed to think about, as long as one had a husband. And she did still have one, since they were still married. But her husband – she walked quietly through the rooms so as not to wake the children, sat in the recliner next to the telephone, and stared into the living room without focussing on anything particular – her husband was in love with another woman, and at that moment – nine-fifteen p.m. – he might be saying to her: You have to be patient. It will take some time. I have to consider my wife and kids. No, he said: I have to consider Edith and the kids. Since they had known each other so long, it would have been natural for them to use her name.

Edith was cold, but she was too tired to get the heater, too tired for anything, even for driving away unsettling thoughts. It was like this every night, and the only thing that helped was taking two sleeping pills. They worked on her like a narcotic, and in the hour or so it took before she fell asleep, she was always feverishly occupied with preparing for the practical arrangements the divorce would bring. But they didn't really interest her all that much. It would work out; she could save money if she had to, which actually was necessary at the moment. Klaus had said that she could have things the way she wanted them, and that everything would be arranged so she and the kids wouldn't have to worry about anything. Everyone must think he's so great! She thought this without bitterness, but also without thinking that he was 'great' herself. That wasn't what she was worried about. She could return to her work with no problem and they wouldn't be dependent on him at all.

Edith sat at his desk in what he called his 'workroom'. There was dust on all the papers and on the month-old piles of newspapers, which no one was allowed to touch, even though they couldn't be of use to him anymore. And as she found a sheet of yellow vellum and pulled out the drawer of pencils and pens, it occurred to her how strange it was that she had never been able to tell anyone what her husband did for a living. Of course she knew he was an assistant professor at a state-run university. Besides that, every Monday morning – up until four months ago – he had sat here writing articles for a magazine whose name she couldn't remember, articles about something which someone phoned about, unless he had left and taken them with him on the eleven o'clock train. These articles he didn't write anymore must have brought in some money. And since it couldn't be entirely cost-free to cultivate an affair with a twenty-something woman, the explanation for the growing pile of unpaid bills was rather obvious.

The sleeping pills started working. She yawned and relaxed her vigilant attitude somewhat. What did she care about all the unpaid bills? Though they did still mean something. He must be in quite a state, her meticulous, conscientious husband, and for a moment she was filled with a strange, impersonal compassion for him. A glimpse of her husband's – her provider's – unknown world flickered across her slightly blurry consciousness. Taxes, accounts, dancing school, a child's coat whose purchase had to be put off till the first. Stains on the wall from dampness which crept higher each year, the loose tiles on the shed roof – all things that had to be taken care of someday, things that chased him from day to day, things he would never get done and could never forget about. He would leave the house to her and the children, the moonlight house which resembled a big chunk of butter, and which could change form, be sliced, scooped out, used up. And now it was suddenly important not to wear things out. They had to be protected, preserved, packed away, as if even a glance could harm them. An old terror erupted inside her at the thought of chair cushions always covered with dark cloth, a living room from which the sunshine was carefully kept out, so the world was in constant twilight. And the expression on her mother's face, as if the final catastrophe was now imminent, when she came home from school with a tear in her dress, or when a pair of shoes couldn't be saved by resoling. But that's not how it would be, or would it? Just in another way that only the children saw?

Edith sat bent over the desk, her blonde hair drooping past

her cheeks like two unkempt bird wings, and she wrote in her childish, ceremonious handwriting: One house, potentially for sale, down payment approx. twenty thousand kroner.

Then she paused and looked at the number. Why is money comforting? A substitute for something else? Men who leave their homes guiltily fling a sack of money over their shoulder to their family without looking back. They pay for their liberation, but in the little side room a child is kneeling, whispering: Dear God, Please let my daddy come back. And in the living room, which has already acquired an indefinable new style, apparent in every place only touched by female hands, her mother sits making plans for the future. The amount he has given her 'once and for all' is to be used for the child's education, so she won't end up in a similar situation. This was the most important thing in the world – and parents, thought Edith, blinded by pride, believe they really know what is most important for their children. Even now there were remnants of this old resentment in her heart. Because wasn't it she who, in an obscure, unexplained way, was right? One morning her mother had said: Little Edith, Daddy has left us. And the world was never whole again, and she was always searching for him. She thought she saw him in all kinds of different places, but when she caught up, out of breath, to the person she was chasing, it was only a stranger. And right now none of this would be so terrifying and fateful, if it hadn't happened back then. Maybe it wouldn't have happened at all, because the thing parents fear for their children might be the very thing the children inevitably gravitate toward, without knowing or meaning to. And since all this was a perpetuation, Edith knew her children would always secretly resent her. They would think it was her fault, no matter what she told them. They would think for all eternity that their father, from some unknown location, was trying to reach them, while their mother, with an adult's horrifying omnipotence, was hindering it.

Edith pushed the paper away and sat motionless, her elbows on the desktop, and her head in her hands. She stared at the sea-green curtain, and the room she was sitting in was like an island of light sailing across a dark, stormy ocean, and she was alone, without a husband, without children, without a future. And then she thought again about the mountains.

'Amazing,' Klaus had said excitedly, adding that he always knew a person would be tremendously moved when they stood face to face with a real mountain for the first time. What had he felt? It was strange she didn't ask. The fact that we are so incredibly uninterested in what is happening inside the person closest to us is probably the source of many problems.

Her eyes started to close, and she could only keep them open with great effort. She had the fleeting sensation that she was getting to be like her mother, and she felt a sort of distant curiosity about her own face. She was surprised that she hadn't noticed deep wrinkles from her nose to her mouth, bitterly tense jaw muscles, and a loose fold of skin under her chin. Her mother must have been so lonely. Why doesn't it dawn on a person that their parents had their own lives separate from their children, until it's too late to ask them how it was? And without knowing that, the whole thing is hidden, the most important thing in the world eternally inaccessible. A tiny hope anxiously made its way through the darkness surrounding her thoughts. What if she told her children the truth? The truth about a father whose love for a woman and tenderness for three children was diminished to a little prick in his conscience when once in a while – because it had to happen – on a street, in a trolley, or on a train, he saw a child who resembled one of them? A little pain that diminished with every embrace, every passionate night, and which in the end disappeared completely in the terrible power radiating from the body of a young, beautiful woman. But is any child in the world able to understand that their father doesn't care? Did she even understand?

Edith was now resting on the messy desktop. Her head was cradled in one elbow, and she heard a faint ringing in her ears. It reminded her of the telephone, which had been cut off because the last bill hadn't been paid. Children love their father at six, eight, and twelve years, and it's still better for them to blame their mother for everything about to happen than to know the truth. What is the truth anyway? Is it so important? The most important thing, thought Edith, is what happens to a person when they see mountains. The most important thing is probably always precisely the thing you can't have. That's where all the happiness is. Was Klaus happy? She started humming a tune: My girl is bright as amber . . . It was what he had sung when shaving that morning, in a high, happy voice. He seemed so incredibly happy that he couldn't hide it. The children were laughing and fooling around with him in the bathroom. And once, once Edith's father had lifted her high up over his head, and she had looked down into his radiant, dark eyes, and without having words for it yet, she understood that in that moment, her big, mild-mannered, melancholy father was happier than she had ever seen him before. Happier for *her* of course, for his little girl, the apple of his eye, who else? This was the last memory she had of him. She had never seen him again. How old had she been? Six or seven. You get by, helped by hate flaring up in your mind like a tall, clear flame, which keeps despair at a distance. Her mother hated the woman, and the child hated the mother, and that was childhood. Her mother died of cancer three years ago, and now Edith was thirty-five, and maybe it is always too late by the time the heart is ready for reconciliation. And it all had something to do with those mountains.

Edith got up and started slowly undressing. She slept in his office; she had been doing that ever since he told her. She wished she could hate the girl and think of her as the one who stole a husband from his wife and a father from his children. But she didn't, which actually was because she only thought of herself as they stood on that narrow, dusty, sunken road in the burning sunshine, staring out toward the long, high mountain range on the other side of the scorched desert, with its sparse, stunted olive trees. She felt overcome with deep disappointment and sadness; she was detached, she had taken this trip in vain, she had sought something that wasn't meant for her. And then she had looked at her husband's ecstatic face and thought: I don't know him; he's a stranger. It was just like when she was a girl and she ran after a man she thought was her father, weaving through the crowd, her heart pounding with glee and fright – only to discover that she was terribly mistaken. And when they returned from their trip, her love had died. That must be how it happened. Why else would she have taken it all so calmly? Because she did take it calmly, if you didn't count that dangerous, brief period of the day after the children had gone to bed, and before he returned from his unknown pleasures. They discussed it calmly and agreed there was no need to hurry the divorce. No tears, no fighting, no hate. It seemed to her now that she had almost been expecting it.

It had arrived like something inevitable, like something destined for the husband she had lost grip of, like a riddle she couldn't solve, like a skein of knitting that was hopelessly tangled. She must have overlooked countless warnings, small signs which attentive women knew to interpret and adjust for, so the impending danger would be averted. But Edith had been completely consumed with her home, her children and her girlfriends, and with her own bird-like, babbling chatter with people who didn't interest her in the least. Hospitality, books about child-rearing, attention to their diet, their teeth, their souls. After the failed vacation she had only really lived through her children and seen things through their eyes. The children's reality. All three of them resembled her. Light skin and hair, with golden freckles around the bridges of their noses; and they had friendly, unhurried dispositions. She often compared them to a couple of pictures she had of herself as a child. When Klaus was in a good mood, he would say: So how are my four girls today? But once in a while it seemed as if he had forgotten them. Edith figured it was because he was busy. She hadn't seen anything; she hadn't noticed anything. He left in the morning and came home in the evening, swinging like a pendulum between two poles, like all other men. And a young woman met him and knew something about him which Edith had forgotten – or maybe never knew. Because we only bring out in others what we need ourselves.

Edith made up the divan and crawled under the comforter, curled up like an infant. She thought: Why did we absolutely have to go on that trip? But she had been looking forward to it as much as he had. They had saved the money – it was before they bought the house. The kids were taken to his parents. She remembered remarkably little about the journey there. Klaus had slept quite a bit on the train through France. And once she had peered carefully at him and was shocked at how old and tired he had come to appear. She had taken his hand and was stroking it, moved by a kind of motherly tenderness, and she had whispered in his ear that soon, soon they would be standing in front of the blue mountains of longing, and they would forget all the gray dust that daily life had strewn over their love. Back then it was natural to say something like that. They had shared their expectations with one another. They had done everything together. They had almost been happy.

Suddenly she whispered into the dark, humming silence: I hope he comes home soon! Her upper lip started trembling slightly, and a deep sigh went through her, the way children sigh after a long, exhausting cry. The sleeping tablets weren't working anymore; they stopped working if she fought long enough against sleeping. She was gripped by the strong urge to tell him that she had felt nothing when she saw those mountains, and that she had no idea what he felt. That it wasn't her fault, and that the children, the three little girls, would be just like her if he didn't stay. No love lasts forever, and he was almost forty-four, and –

Her heart was hammering, and she sat up, listening to the street. A key was put in the lock. He was here! She slid quietly out of bed and tiptoed to the living room, but he had gone upstairs to the bedroom. Edith put on her housecoat, and without really knowing what she was going to say to him, she followed him barefoot, and opened the door just as he was pulling down his suspenders from his shoulders. His jacket was already over the back of a chair. He looked surprised at her and opened his mouth to say something. But as if she were afraid of what it would be, she stammered out quickly:

'Sorry, I didn't realize it was so late.'

He smiled awkwardly at her, and stopped undressing.

'I know,' he said. 'It's always later than you think.'

And even though he probably didn't mean anything by them, his words kept echoing inside Edith through the years, long after the three little girls had grown up, and gotten married, and come by for infrequent, dutiful visits with their divorced mother. Would something change in their hearts if they ever got to see real mountains? Edith never knew.

The Trouble with Happiness

When I was seventeen we moved into a three-room apartment, to what my mother called 'a better neighborhood'.
The monthly rent was twenty kroner more than the old two-
room apartment we used to live in. My father was sure it
would ruin us, but my mother had gotten it into her head
that we were going to move. She gave no justification for her
idea, and my father couldn't fight it. My brother had married shortly before, just to get out of the house. Maybe my
mother thought I would stay home longer if I had my own
room. But I had my room no more to myself than I had had
in the old apartment. It was only mine when I was sleeping on the divan which used to be in my parents' bedroom.
Only a cretonne curtain separated my room from what my
mother called 'the sitting room', which was intended for
guests. But no one ever visited us except Aunt Anna. She
was the sweetest and most cheerful person in all my childhood, but at that time I was only interested in young men and
poetry. My mother considered both of these hostile elements
in our family. All my poems were about love, and when she
got hold of one of them, she burst into tears and said she

couldn't understand where I had been exposed to such disgusting ideas.

The apartment was in a corner building, and along one of the streets there actually was a semblance of propriety, which consisted of some stucco on the gloomy facades and somewhat fewer snotty children in the street than we were used to. On the corner there was a cafe, where there were constant fights and disturbances. And along the building's other side, the street was exactly like the one we had moved away from. But we had lived in the rear before, which I only now realized was a huge advantage to me. Now my mother was able to sit lurking in my bedroom, ready to throw open the window as soon as I came home at night with a young man, to whom I would say a tender goodbye at the front door.

'So, there you are finally!' she would yell. 'Get in here right now!'

All the young men got scared and hurried away before we were able to make a next date. When I went in (we lived on the first floor), she was standing there in her flowered cotton nightgown staring at me with angry, sleepless eyes.

'You are becoming a woman of the streets,' she said.

She always used expressions like that, sometimes interspersing them with biblical quotations, though she didn't believe in God or the devil. Never in my life did I long for something so much as I did then – to turn eighteen so I could move out. I had a job at a warehouse where I packed tin boxes eight hours a day. For that I received twenty-five kroner a week, and I gave twenty to my mother. After we had eaten dinner, my father would lie down on the divan for a nap, and my mother would sit down to knit with furious movements. Although my father always slept for a couple of hours after dinner, she took it as a personal insult. She complained that my brother never came home and visited, but when he did make a rare appearance, he brought his wife and my mother would ignore her. I sat paging through the newspaper while I gathered the courage to say I was going to the movies with a girlfriend. Then things would get so quiet between us it seemed noisy if I swallowed. Usually I waited until my father was awake to say something like that. Sometimes he took my side, though I'm sure he paid dearly for it afterward.

Then a whole lot of things happened at once, but since they happened while I was deeply infatuated with a young mechanic with a motorcycle, I barely noticed them. First, Aunt Anna's husband was admitted to the hospital. He was rarely mentioned in our household, because he drank and was supported by his wife. Aunt Anna was a seamstress and she often visited us on her way home, after she had dropped off some finished work at the company that she sewed for. When she visited, she and my mother laughed like two young girls, and my mother was like a different person. Maybe that was what she used to be like. Maybe she should have married a different husband and lived a very different life. In any case, I have only seen her happy when Aunt Anna was visiting. She was her only sister. Aunt Anna always kept her hat on because she only meant to stay 'a brief moment', as if the hat would contradict the truth, when she eventually left, that she had stayed several hours. My parents didn't hide the fact that they hoped her husband would die. They wished it for her sake. To me her visits meant it was easier to slip out in the evening, because now my parents had something to talk about. Her husband did eventually die, and at the burial my aunt cried as if she were being whipped. I cried too, God knows why, because I had never met him. Afterward we went to a rather nice pub and had coffee. Not fifteen minutes had passed before my mother and my Aunt Anna were breathless with laughter over some occurrence from their childhood. My aunt had beautiful teeth with no cavities, which was highly unusual in my family. When we left the pub, my brother came over to me and said, 'Lisa took off with another man. And I'm living in a room in Larslejstræde.' He said it as if it didn't affect him one bit, and I thought that was how it was. 'Don't tell our parents,' he said, and I promised. Outside, my mechanic was waiting on his red motorcycle, and I sat down behind him without saying good-bye to anyone, because when my mother was around Aunt Anna, she forgot about everything else.

My aunt began to visit more frequently, which softened my mother's mood and gave me more freedom. She lost interest in calling me inside from my nightly embraces. My mechanic's name was Kurt, and I started to visit his parents, who were very friendly toward me. We exchanged rings at their house, so we were engaged for real, and I began to feel awkward about never inviting him to my home. I didn't know what I should do. My mother never wanted us to be close to people outside our family. She never wanted us to grow up. Above all, she didn't want us to team up with a member of the opposite sex. Perhaps she never wanted to have children, and perhaps nothing ever happened to her in this world that she really wanted. I couldn't explain something as strange as that to Kurt. I could have asked Aunt Anna to talk some sense into my mother, if I had some way of contacting her that didn't involve my mother. My aunt was childless, though she loved my brother and me. But my mother had always made sure we had no direct contact with her. When we were young, we were never allowed to visit because of her drunken husband. I didn't even know exactly where she lived.

While I was speculating over this problem, my mother

came by one day to fetch me from work. I could see on her face that something terrible had happened. As we were walking home, she told me that my aunt was in the hospital. She had started bleeding, and by my mother's hints I understood that she was too old for that. 'So it has to be cancer,' decided my mother with a wavering voice. 'If she dies, I will have no reason to go on living.' On the corner of Valdemarsgade and Enghavevej, Kurt was straddling his motorcycle, and he revved it in anticipation. He always waited for me there. I shook my head as a sign that he shouldn't make himself known, furious at my mother, who was now leaning heavily on my arm, as if she suddenly had grown old and would fall down if I let go. I was also furious at myself for being a head taller than her. I was furious at my entire childhood. It was as if it would never end, and my strides felt stiff and awkward as we walked past my fiancé, whose red motorcycle and shiny leather jacket were gleaming in the autumn sunshine. My engagement ring, which was bought on installment, was in my shoulder bag. I didn't have the nerve to wear it at home.

As if there were no end to misfortunes, my father lost his job shortly after my aunt's admittance to the hospital. My mother found out that my brother's wife had run off, and began basing our entire future around his moving back in with us. I didn't really listen when she told me about her plan, and she asked me to talk him into it. I was always waiting for the chance to see Kurt at his home, where everything was happy and normal. But at the same time I had sent some poems to a magazine, because I wasn't planning to package tin boxes for the rest of my life. I felt I simply could not continue living two lives, and deep in my heart I was starting to doubt if a mechanic was a suitable husband for a writer. In any case I became less excited about having Kurt visit my family. It became more difficult anyway, since now my father always sat on my divan reading an old encyclopedia, and I only had my room to myself at night. We didn't have enough money to heat more than one room, and we had to have our coats on just to stay warm. My father's unemployment check and my weekly twenty kroner were only enough to keep the worst misery from our door. I would turn eighteen in a few months, and gradually I realized that the only salvation for *me* would be if my brother moved back home. But he never visited us, and when I thought about our plan, I felt bad for him. It was the only generous feeling I preserved in the conscious iciness I was building up against my family. That was why I kept postponing my visit to his rented room.

My aunt had an operation, and people at the hospital told her she would soon make a full recovery, but that she would need to be nursed and cared for until she regained her strength. Did she have any family she could live with? My mother was more than excited for her to come and live with us, and she was installed in my father's bed. Then he had to sleep on the lumpy sofa in the ice-cold living room, and I woke constantly to his snoring through the thin curtain, until I got used to it. Now there was another mouth to feed, but, as it turned out, it didn't matter, because my aunt was too sick to eat. My mother spent all her time at the bedside, and in the beginning we could hear their continual, familiar chuckling and babbling from the bedroom. My father resumed his habit of sleeping a couple of hours after dinner, now that my mother's reproachful stare didn't force him to sit paging for hours through the old encyclopedia. I could go wherever I wanted. But I didn't go anywhere, because I had received a reply from the magazine. They wanted to publish two of my poems, which the editor found 'extremely promising', As if with the wave of a magic wand, this message changed my entire identity, my entire outlook on life. It occurred to me that everything I had loved about Kurt wouldn't work in the elite literary circle in which I would soon be moving. Within a few days I sloughed off my infatuation and got invited to dinner by the editor of the magazine, and in a fog of newfound pride I received my termination notice from the tin box company, after the president had discovered me in the attic in the middle of writing a poem on brown packing paper. I hurried out to the editor, an unmarried, middle-aged man, the type who loved to be surrounded by young people. He comforted me by saying that I could definitely live by my pen, and if I ran into trouble, he had always seen it as his mission to support the arts.

All this was impossible to talk about at home. My father had found some temporary work, and he started staying out late. Presumably he went to a bar, because he was completely superfluous in my mother's world. That is how I finally had my room to myself, in peace, and I read books and wrote poems until late into the night. I spent daytimes in the reading room at the library, so my mother would think I was at work, and the money I got for the published poems was locked in the sewing box with the inlaid mother-of-pearl, my brother's journeyman test piece, which he had given me at my confirmation. It was a very pretty little thing. When the lid opened, it played: *Fight for all you hold dear* . . . At any rate those were the lyrics I sang inwardly to the crisp melody.

One evening the doorbell rang, and it was Kurt with his tight leather jacket and his crash helmet on his head, requesting in no uncertain terms to have a word with me. As I let him inside, feeling rather flustered, my mother opened the bedroom door and yelled, 'Get the doctor quick. She's in a lot of pain. Tell him to come right away. Who is that?'

Without answering, I pushed Kurt back out the door, explaining about my sick aunt and asking him to drive me to the doctor. He sped off at breakneck speed, which didn't impress me anymore. While we rode, he told me it was over and that he was going to date any girl he wanted. I don't know if I even answered, but outside the doctor's stairway, he held up his right hand in front of my face so I could see that he had removed his ring. It seemed to me that he was behaving ridiculously, and I thought about my editor, who understood writing and had the means to support it. But I had no interest in explaining this to Kurt. All I wanted was to be done with him. For some reason he walked with me up to the doctor, who had examined my aunt before. 'Dear God,' he said, when he heard why I was there. 'Well, then, I guess it won't be long now.' Then I understood for the first time that my aunt was going to die. Did she know that? Did my mother know that? When Kurt drove me home again, I asked him to wait outside while I went in and got my engagement ring. He took it hesitantly, and I noticed the sorrow in his face, which was no longer my problem. I never saw him again, and I soon forgot all about him.

My aunt's cheerfulness declined, and my mother was getting tired of sitting with her. When I was home, she pleaded with me to take her place. The window in the bedroom faced a closed courtyard with a bicycle shed, and on its roof roosted cats, raising their loving yowls to the heavens. The cafe's back door faced the courtyard, and the drunkest guests were always let out that way. When I opened the window, the smell of vomit and cat urine wafted in to my aunt, but it wasn't as bad as the rotten smell that had begun to spread from her bed. I don't think she noticed it herself. She looked terrible. Her bright red gums were always exposed, even when she was sleeping, and her yellowed, emaciated fingers continually groped the comforter, as if they were searching for something. Twice a day a nurse arrived to give her a morphine injection. Soon after she had it, she started whispering, without turning her head, unaware whether it was my mother or me beside her. I had to bend right over her to hear what she was saying. The oppressive smell took my breath away. She whispered about clothes she had sewn for my mother's dolls, and about their experiences as young girls. When she wanted to laugh, it turned into a violent coughing attack. 'Do you remember,' she murmured, 'when you hid the barber in the clothes closet? If Niels hadn't left so quickly, he might have suffocated.' Niels was my father. I started laughing, because I laughed a lot in those days. Then my aunt realized she had the wrong audience, and she quickly started whispering about all the dresses she had sewn for me when I was a little girl.

My mother was sitting in my bedroom, sobbing into her apron.

'How much longer?' she asked. 'God help us, may she soon find redemption.'

Maybe I could have comforted her if she had expressed herself less bombastically. To me it seemed to make her grief appear unauthentic. In my judgmental mood and at my age it also seemed abnormal for her to be so tightly bound to her sister when she had a husband and children.

Not long after, my father lost his job again, and my mother scraped margarine on our bread and we had porridge three times a week. It was a terribly cold winter, and my aunt still refused to die. They thought I was still packaging tin boxes, because, thanks to my editor, I was still able to deliver my weekly twenty kroner to my family.

One month before I turned eighteen, I pulled myself

together and visited my brother at his room on Larslejstræde. The landlord looked at me skeptically when I asked to see my brother. 'They all say that,' she said acerbically, and let me in. He stood in the center of the floor in a nearly empty room, in the process of gluing together a chair. A sudden wave of tenderness came over me at the sight of him. I hadn't seen him in such a long time. He seemed to be glad to see me too, and we sat down on his unmade bed.

'Dad doesn't have any work,' I said, 'and Aunt Anna is dying, and they're flat broke.'

'I don't see what that has to do with me,' he said defiantly. 'They ruined things between me and Gunhild. I could never invite a girl home without Mom going bananas. At least here we can be in peace.'

'Do you have a new one?' I asked, a bit shocked. I hadn't thought of that possibility, even though he was twenty-one and a handsome young man.

'Yes,' he said. 'And I plan on keeping her.'

To my surprise I started sobbing. He had never seen me do that. We never expressed our feelings. That was how it was at home. He put his arm around my shoulder, which was also the first time ever. Then the confessions poured out of me, about my broken-off engagement, about not packaging tin boxes anymore, about the poems and my plans for the future, and about the editor, who seemed to be in love with me, and who had enough influence to help me make it in the world. And all this, I explained, could only unfold if he moved back home. If one of us didn't support them economically, they would both freeze and starve. If nothing else, I pleaded, he could just do it temporarily to ease the transition when I moved out.

He stood up and started pacing in the little room.

'Do you make money off that – writing?' he asked sheepishly.

'Nothing to speak of,' I said, 'but I will eventually. And then I promise to help them.'

A sad smile emerged in his brown eyes.

'Fine, fine,' he said with a sigh. 'I'll do it. Just stop crying. I can't stand it. I think you're going to be famous. Just wait, that editor is going to marry you.'

I didn't look at him when I said goodbye. I didn't ask who he was engaged to. I knew he would never be able to invite her home to our parents. Ours wasn't a family that could ever accept new members.

I moved into a rented room three days after my aunt died. My mother was too heartbroken to really notice. I took advantage of her condition to tell her I was going to be married soon. She answered strangely: It doesn't matter who you marry.

I never really understood what she meant by that.

My brother kept his promise and moved back home to the room behind the cretonne curtain, and I forgot all about them – forgot about my home, and lived my own life.

But sometimes – when someone has left me, or I discover inadvertently in the eyes of my children a glimpse of cold observation, of merciless, unsurmountable distance, I take out my brother's pretty little sewing case and slowly open the mother-of-pearl inlaid lid. *Fight for all you hold dear*, plays the worn old music maker, and an unnamed sadness swells inside my mind, because they are all dead or disappeared, and my brother and I no longer communicate.